11 - 11

Martha

**Center Point
Large Print**

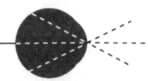

**This Large Print Book carries the
Seal of Approval of N.A.V.H.**

Martha

Diana Wallis Taylor

CENTER POINT LARGE PRINT
THORNDIKE, MAINE

This Center Point Large Print edition is published
in the year 2011 by arrangement with
Revell, a division of Baker Publishing Group.

The text of this Large Print edition is unabridged.
In other aspects, this book may
vary from the original edition.
Printed in the United States of America.
Set in 16-point Times New Roman type.

ISBN: 978-1-61173-228-3

Library of Congress Cataloging-in-Publication Data

Taylor, Diana Wallis, 1938–
Martha / Diana Wallis Taylor. — Center Point large print ed.
p. cm.
ISBN 978-1-61173-228-3 (library binding : alk. paper)
1. Martha, Saint—Fiction. 2. Women in the Bible—Fiction.
3. Bible. N.T.—History of Biblical events—Fiction.
4. Large type books. I. Title.
PS3620.A942M38 2011b
813′.6—dc22
                                                      2011030013

To those women who, because of our feminine
gift of multitasking,
have become "Marthas."
May they each find, as her sister Mary did,
that "good place that shall not be taken away,"
at the feet of the Savior.

Martha

1

Martha watched her father walk slowly up the road as the afternoon shadows appeared, and he was smiling. Ephraim looked tired but pleased. At his raised hand of greeting she hurried to meet him. Bursting with curiosity, she nearly danced beside him as they returned to the house. A dozen questions whirled in her head, but she held them in, knowing her father would tell her in his own time.

He looked past her. "And where is Mary?"

Martha swallowed her impatience. "She helped me in the garden this morning. I asked her to wash the vegetables." She hoped the task was done, for Mary, at ten, was a dreamer and easily distracted.

Ephraim put a hand on her shoulder. "You are teaching her well, daughter."

She beamed at his praise, but her question tumbled out in spite of her good intentions. "You have news, Abba?"

He smiled and nodded, his eyes twinkling. "My offer is being considered and they will let me know soon. I believe I presented you in a most favorable light. Phineas is a worthy young man and an only son. He is strong and helps his father in the fields. Gera and his wife, Rhumah, are

9

good people. You would have a pleasant home."

Martha could hardly contain her excitement. She was fifteen and her father had gone to arrange a marriage for her. She could soon be betrothed. Reaching up, she put a hand on her father's cheek. "Thank you, Abba. When will we know?"

Her dark eyes sparkled as she looked up at her father. She was taller than most of the other girls in Bethany, nearly reaching her father's shoulder. She'd bound up the auburn hair that flowed in gentle cascades down her back, under her shawl. While she turned a few heads when she walked through the village, her father told her many times, "Beauty does not run the home, daughter, only skillful hands." Her hands were indeed skillful, for she had learned to help her mother in the household duties when she was even younger than Mary.

Her father tipped her chin up with his finger. "Gera told me we will talk after the Sabbath."

Martha sighed. She would just have to wait.

It had been two years since her mother died. She did her best to care for their home. Her father and her twelve-year-old brother Lazarus helped as they could, but the burden fell on Martha. Her father hadn't remarried. She worried about the pains in his stomach that troubled him from time to time.

"I fear I'm a poor risk for a husband—a man given to weak spells, with three children," he told her upon more than one occasion.

Martha knew of two women in Bethany who had indicated they might be interested, but Ephraim would not commit himself. Perhaps now, if she were to be betrothed, her father would consider taking a wife to be a mother to Mary and Lazarus. Yet, even as she thought of this, she felt a twinge of guilt. When her mother's mantle as the woman of the household had fallen on her shoulders that dark day, she had promised to take care of her brother and sister. It seemed so urgent at the time. If she married and left, would she be breaking her promise?

Her father went to have Nathan the blacksmith sharpen his sickle for the coming wheat harvest while Martha checked the oil lamps to be sure they were filled. Earlier in the day she had done the washing and now gathered the dried clothing to bring it inside.

Their house was made of brick strengthened with straw and plastered over with lime and clay. Ephraim was a brick-maker and was teaching Lazarus how to make sturdy bricks of clay and straw, which they sold to others in the village. He also repaired roofs and walls for those who could not do it themselves. The house was cool in the summer and warm during the cold rains of the winter months. The roof of reeds and sticks coated with thick clay kept out the rain but needed to be maintained constantly.

One large room in the house served as the living, dining, and sleeping room with the family's pallets rolled up and stored in a corner. The weather was still pleasant, so Martha had Mary set the table in the courtyard. Looking at the leaves of the trees that were beginning to turn, she knew they would soon have to move the cooking brazier inside. She frowned. That would be necessary, but she didn't like the way the smoke filled their small house. While the weather was good, they ate at the table in the courtyard. When the weather turned cold, Martha brought their small brazier inside for cooking, and they ate there. While Martha, Lazarus, and Mary slept in the main room, there was a smaller room that had been added to the house when her father brought Martha's mother, Jerusha, there as a bride. Since her mother died, her father slept there alone.

Martha prepared the vegetables and baked a chicken with onions and garlic for their Sabbath dinner. A lentil stew simmered in a pot over the fire. She added some rue. Fat, purple figs, the first of the season, were piled in a basket on the table, and slices of fresh cucumber shimmered in a bowl. They must eat early, for no work could be done when the Sabbath began at sunset.

A soft breeze passed through the courtyard, swirling the leaves, but there was no moisture in it, and she knew the season of *hamsin,* the dry winds, was beginning. It was the month of Sivan, and after the Sabbath the wheat harvest would begin. The men of the village would help Ephraim with his harvest and he in turn would help others. Martha and Lazarus would be put to work in the fields bundling up the sheaves of grain. Adah, a woman too old to help in the fields, had asked for Mary to help her watch two or three small children who were too young to help with the har-vest.

Lazarus came into the courtyard with a bundle of twigs for the fire. He was a sturdy boy, already showing evidence that he would be tall like his father. How proud she was of the man he was becoming. And he did his chores without com-plaint or prodding, like milking the goats early each morning and feeding the donkey.

He put down the bundle and lay a few twigs on the flames.

"Mary, could you ladle the milk for supper?" Martha asked as she pulled several cups from the cupboard and set them near the crock that stood in the coolest corner of the house. They had fresh milk daily, thanks to Lazarus's early-morning routine of milking the goats.

Martha turned back to the small cupboard to get some bowls, but Mary stood motionless, holding an unwashed cucumber. She was looking up at a flock of sparrows.

Martha sighed heavily. "Mary, finish the vegetables. We must store them quickly. The

Sabbath approaches. I have other things to do, I can't do those too."

Mary was instantly repentant, her face downcast at Martha's sharp tone of voice.

As her younger sister diligently resumed her task, Martha regretted her words. She had been too cross with Mary lately. She wondered if she could even remember when she had time to daydream herself. She had taken her mother's place at such a young age. Did her responsibilities ever end? She got a basket from the storeroom and began to help Mary place the vegetables in it. Mary gave her a shy smile of forgiveness. How many times her younger sister's gentle disposition offset her own impulsive one.

With sunset approaching, the family gathered as Martha lit the Sabbath candles, closed her eyes, and passed her hands over the bright flames. Then she covered her eyes with her hands and murmured the prayer that had been passed down to her people through the ages, "Blessed are you, Lord our God, King of the Universe, Who has made us holy through his commandments and commanded us to kindle the Sabbath lights."

Then, as the sun sank behind the Judean hills and the evening stars began to appear, the three muted blasts of the shofar, the ram's horn, sounded from the Temple Mount a mile and a half away, marking the beginning of the Sabbath and calling the faithful to prayer.

Martha had put out the fire under the stove before the shofar sounded. Now she placed their still warm supper on the low table and basked in Ephraim's nod of approval.

He poured the wine into the Kiddush cup and held it up.

As Martha listened to her father intoning the familiar prayers, she wondered what it would be like to listen to Phineas say the prayers in their household. Then she chided herself for foolish daydreams. It would not be Phineas, it would be his father, since they would live with her husband's family. A small shadow passed over her thoughts. She would be only a helper to her new mother-in-law, not in charge of the household. Perhaps it would just be like helping her mother again. She looked out over the courtyard. Who would take her place here?

Her thoughts were brought quickly back to the present as she took the Kiddush cup Lazarus was passing to her. She took a sip and handed it to Mary, who received it with reverence.

Ephraim broke the traditional *challah* bread into chunks to dip into the sauce. As they ate, Ephraim quizzed Lazarus on what he had learned from the rabbi that week and Martha listened respectfully to his recitations.

Watching her young sister nibble daintily at her piece of chicken, Martha thought there would be no difficulty finding her sister a husband one day. She was a pretty child. Her eyes, like her brother's, were from her father's side of the family, wide and dark in a smooth olive complexion.

When their Sabbath meal was over, they bowed their heads and Ephraim spoke the final prayer.

With the ceremonies of Friday evening over, Mary and Lazarus settled down on their pallets and were asleep in moments. Martha looked outside and saw that her father was sitting quietly in the courtyard, contemplating the night sky. While she left him alone with his thoughts, she also looked up into the night sky.

"Oh, God Who Sees me, may there be good news tomorrow." Then she sighed. It was for God to determine her way. Instantly repentant, she prayed instead for the will of God in her life and went to her pallet.

The next morning upon awakening, Martha spoke the blessing and rose to prepare for their trip into Jerusalem to the Temple Mount for Sabbath prayers. It was a short walk, within the two-mile limit for a Sabbath journey. Ephraim in earlier years carried Mary on his shoulders, but now she walked beside him.

As they approached from the east and rounded a turn in the road, the city, hidden by the ridge of Olivet, burst into view. Martha never tired of the first glimpse of Jerusalem. The Temple was still hidden until they crossed Ophel, the suburb of the priests, then finally the panorama of the whole city stretched before them. Dark valleys and hills, the walls, towers, palaces, and streets of the city surrounded the Temple. As the sunlight caught its walls, the Temple stood like a mighty fortress, dwarfing the surrounding buildings. The sight never ceased to delight her. A rush of joy filled her heart as she gazed at the familiar scene.

They began their ascent into the city, and Martha noticed the increased number of Roman soldiers stationed along the road and near the steps leading up to the Temple. She remembered hearing her father and one of their neighbors furtively comment on the heavy taxes they were required to pay to the Roman government.

Ephraim had shaken his head solemnly. "The amount increases each year. We have no say. It is a burden that leaves us little to live on."

"We have waited hundreds of years for the Messiah to come and deliver us from our oppressors," their neighbor Shaul said. "Now is a good time for him to come?"

The Messiah. The Chosen One. Would he come in her lifetime? Each Jewish mother who gave birth to a son hoped beyond hope that he would be the one who would free their people. Martha thought of this. If she were to marry and have a son, could he be the one? She reined in her thoughts and concentrated on where she was walking, lest she stumble on the uneven stones of the passage.

As Martha and her family passed by, the Roman soldiers stood watching the people with sneers of distaste. The Romans and the Jews had no love for one another.

One soldier watched Martha and his eyes narrowed into a leer as she passed by. She looked down at the ground and made sure she and Mary stayed close to their father.

As they approached the Temple, Martha looked around at families moving up into the Temple courtyard and was glad it was a Sabbath service and not Passover. The roads were less crowded with people. Those whose villages were within the prescribed two miles of travel on the Sabbath could come to the Temple. Being close to Jerusalem, Bethany had no need for a synagogue, as did towns farther away.

"Ephraim. All is well with you?"

Martha turned at the familiar deep voice of their friend, Nathan the blacksmith. His wife, Rhoda, was frail and spent much of her time on her pallet complaining about her health. Nathan had hired an elderly widow in the village who came in to help with cooking and the household chores for a few coins. He and his wife had no children and the women of Bethany clucked their tongues. How had he offended God, they murmured, to have such calamity fall upon him?

With his shy manner and tendency to keep to himself, he discouraged friendships, but Martha's father had befriended him and had gone out of his way to be kind to a man he knew to be lonely.

Nathan, in his late twenties, was an imposing figure as he strode through their village. Now, as he stood before them, his Sabbath clothes did little to conceal the muscles on his arms.

"I am well, my friend. It is a good day, is it not?"

Nathan nodded, his face serious. "You are here with your fine family." He stroked his thick beard and rocked on his heels, clearing his throat.

Martha had heard through other women in the village that he was uncomfortable around women. She resisted a smile. He was obviously uncomfortable now.

Ephraim looked at each of his children. "Yes, a fine family. I am blessed."

Mary was restless and Martha didn't wish to be rude to a neighbor. She looked pointedly at her father.

Her father put his hand on Nathan's shoulder. "Let us walk together to the Temple."

Nathan nodded to Martha and Mary and quickly turned away with Ephraim and Lazarus.

With Mary walking quickly to keep up with her, Martha hurried into the Court of the Women. She paused briefly and glanced back to watch as Ephraim, Lazarus, and Nathan climbed the stone steps to the Court of the Israelites. She must make it a point to call on Nathan's wife, Rhoda. Perhaps she could take them some of her lentil stew.

Just then, to her delight, she spotted Phineas and his father, Gera, moving with the group of men. They did not see her and her heart fluttered as she drew her shawl closer around her face to watch Phineas unobtrusively as he followed his father. He was handsome indeed. She struggled to keep her mind on her prayers and had to force herself to concentrate on the reading from the Torah portion for the week, and the reading from the Prophets. As she listened, she found herself wondering about these promises of the Redeemer who was to come.

The service ended, and the men and women milled about, finding their families as they exited the temple. Martha looked for Phineas and his father, but they were lost in the crowd. She hoped her father had been able to talk to Gera. Mary loved coming to the Temple, and her eyes were bright as she watched everything. Martha urged her toward their usual meeting place by the entrance to wait for her father and brother. When they came, Nathan was no longer with them.

It was a pleasant day, and they walked leisurely home. The spring flowers were in bloom, and Mary stopped to pick some as they walked. Blue cornflowers and scarlet anemones covered the sides of the road and were interspersed with crops in the fields in colorful profusion. When they reached their home, Martha sent Mary to find a clay vase to put them in. The flowers gave their table a festive look. She gave Mary a brief smile, letting her know she was pleased, as she placed the cold noonday meal of leftovers on their table. Mary, tired from the long walk, rubbed her eyes and finally rested on her pallet.

With a quiet afternoon ahead of her, Martha drew her shawl over her head and walked outside the gate, free at least for one day from household work. She sat on a rock and watched the clouds moving lazily across the sky. The burden of taking her mother's place weighed on her spirit. If she married, she would take on the additional burden of another family, and then children. She sighed. How long had it been since she had been just a child, playing games with her friends? She rose and walked to her favorite place, the quiet and shady Mount of Olives. She strolled among the gnarled trees, long since stripped of their harvest, and put her hand on one of the trunks. How long had they grown there—long before her father, as long as her family could remember? A peaceful feeling settled over her as she walked in the garden and listened to the lively chatter of the sparrows as they flitted among the branches.

Her thoughts turned again to Phineas. She had seen him many times in the village but had never had the courage to speak to him. Her father had decided he was a good choice for her, but she didn't really know him very well. In any case, if they were betrothed, they would come to know each other better. There were some young men in the village she did not wish to marry, and she was glad her father sought a good husband for her.

Lost in her thoughts, she suddenly realized the sun was fading and the afternoon shadows were growing long. Her short time of solitude was ending, yet, as always, she felt rested as she rose to return home.

As she neared their home, she saw the blacksmith walking down the road away from the house. He must have stopped by for one of his infrequent visits with her father. For a moment she wondered if his wife was well enough to say the Sabbath prayers. As large as the man was, his size seemed diminished as he slowly walked alone toward his home. She watched him a moment more and then opened the gate to the courtyard of her home.

Martha helped her family prepare for the time of separation and the end of Sabbath. Her father took Mary's hand and the four of them looked at the night sky where three stars were bright and visible. It was a reminder that God watched over them and cared about their daily lives. They went back into the house to say the prayers for havdalah.

Martha listened to the familiar words, but her mind wandered again. Would she be afraid when she became a bride?

Her father lifted the Kiddush cup the first time and spoke the blessing over the wine.

When it was time to light the braided havdalah candle, the first act of work on the Sabbath, Martha held her hands close to the flame that represented the light by which she worked with her hands. "Blessed are you, Lord our God, King of the universe, Creator of the light of fire," she said softly. Her father and brother did the same.

Ephraim picked up the Kiddush cup again and blessed it. Then he spilled a small amount of the wine on an earthen plate, symbolizing the loss of Sabbath. Each of them drank from their cups of wine. The havdalah candle was finally extinguished as Ephraim dipped it into his wine. They sat in the darkness a moment, and then Mary, in a high, clear voice, began the song of the prophet Elijah and they joined in.

Tomorrow would be a day of hard work and they would need a good night's rest. They rose from the table and each wished the other *"Shavua tov,"* a good week ahead, and went to their pallets for the night. Martha lay quietly for a long time, her mind turning with thoughts of the coming day. If she were betrothed, she would have a year to prepare for the wedding. She was curious as to what went on between a bridegroom and his bride on the wedding night. At moments like these, she wished desperately for her mother. Martha missed her singing and gentle hands. She had so many questions, but now there was no one to answer them.

Closing her eyes, she sighed happily. The wheat harvest would begin tomorrow. And Gera had promised to speak to her father.

2

Martha sat up and stretched. After a brief morning prayer, she looked over at Lazarus, who lay rubbing his eyes. Dawn was just breaking, pushing away the shadows of the night.

Ephraim entered the main room and glanced at Lazarus. "Rise, my children, we have work to do."

Martha sprang up quickly and shook her younger sister awake. There was food to prepare and pack for the midday break.

Lazarus yawned and rose also. When her father and brother started for the fields, Martha went to the gate with Mary as her sister prepared to walk to the house of Adah. She would be helping Adah take care of the smallest children while their parents worked in the fields.

"You must mind Adah, Mary, and be a help to her. We'll see you at the end of the day."

Mary loved children and Martha knew she was looking forward to helping Adah. Mary's face was alight at the day's prospects and she started to skip, humming a little song to herself. Then she glanced back at Martha's pursed lips and, with a sigh, began to walk more sedately.

Martha hurried to the fields to help her brother bundle the grain after the reapers. She would not see Phineas, as he would be helping his father in their own fields.

Neighbors shouted greetings to one another as they began the work of the day. The men were already perspiring as the brief coolness of the morning receded and the sun rose higher in the sky. Some cut the wheat, some gathered it for the threshing floor. Other young boys and girls helped as Martha and Lazarus did, tying the sheaves into bundles to be picked up. As she worked, Martha heard the women murmuring among themselves. Her eyes widened as she listened.

"There is news, Zillah. Did you know that Simon, the husband of Judith, returned from working on the last caravan and discovered a large white spot on his arm?"

"Oh, Huldah, could it be?" Zillah, the potter's wife, murmured.

The first woman lowered her voice, but Martha caught the words.

"It might be, oh, can I even say the word?"

"You mean leprosy?" Zillah whispered in horror.

There was a shocked silence, then the two

women murmured among themselves.

Suddenly Huldah turned and saw Martha and Lazarus listening. She tilted her head toward them and with a meaningful nod moved on along the row of wheat.

Lazarus stood still, his eyes wide. "Sister, did they say leprosy?"

She looked after the women, her mouth suddenly dry. "I think so. I pray it is not true. That would be terrible for his family." Heaviness settled on her heart. Simon's daughter, Esther, was her best friend.

Lazarus hung his head. "I cannot think how I would feel if it were Abba."

At the midday break, the workers gathered together to eat a brief meal and rest. Anna, the local midwife, who also cared for the sick with her bag of herbs, brought a large jug of water on her shoulder and the workers passed the cup, drinking deeply after the long hours working in the heat.

Martha told Ephraim what she had heard, and Lazarus, sitting next to his father, stared solemnly out over the fields. He looked up finally. "Is there a cure for leprosy, Abba?"

"It will depend on the form it has taken. The God of all the earth knows all things, my son. He is able to cleanse Simon and we must trust him to do so if he wills it." Ephraim looked down at his son's frowning face. "Is there another matter that troubles you?"

Lazarus lowered his voice. "Will Simon have to live away from his family?"

Ephraim nodded solemnly. "It will depend on the words of the priest. Simon must go to the priest to be examined."

Martha shuddered. She prayed the priest would not find one in their village with leprosy. Still thinking of Esther, she asked, "Abba, what will his family do?"

Ephraim put a hand on her shoulder. "God will provide, and we will help them, as we do for those in need in our village."

Their conversation was interrupted by the sound of a young boy calling Ephraim's name. It was Joab, the son of their neighbor, Shaul. He ran breathlessly across the fields waving his hands.

Joab caught his breath and then blurted out, "Adah sent me for you. It is Mary. She has been hurt."

Ephraim sought out Anna, who was preparing to return to the village with her water jug. She nodded. "I will go and get my healing bag and meet you at the house of Adah."

Lazarus would have come with them, but Ephraim shook his head. "You will be more help to remain in our field. The men will need you here. Your sister and I will see to Mary."

He nodded reluctantly and turned back toward the field as Martha and her father hurried to the village. They found Mary lying on a pallet, sobbing with pain. Her left leg showed a huge bulge and the skin was turning purple. To Martha, it appeared broken, but at least no bone protruded through the skin.

Adah sputtered apologies. "One moment she was talking with the children and the next moment she was lying in the courtyard."

Ephraim looked down at Adah, his face stern. "You did not see what happened?"

The older woman looked away. She spread her hands and shrugged. "Something about a bird, the children said . . ."

Ephraim turned to Joab and the other children. "What happened here?"

One of the children stepped forward, her eyes wide with fear. "It was a baby bird. It fell out of its nest." The other children nodded solemnly.

"Mary climbed the tree to put it back," said Joab.

Martha caught her father's eye. Mary was tenderhearted when it came to small creatures, and also impulsive. He sighed deeply. They both knew it was something Mary would do.

Mary's sobs of pain tore Martha's heart as she cradled her young sister gently and rocked her, crooning softly with words of comfort.

"I didn't know she'd climbed the tree," Adah murmured defensively. "I heard her cry out, but I was in the house. How could I get to her in time?"

Anna walked swiftly into the courtyard and squatted down to examine Mary's leg. With practiced fingers she probed the wound, now swelling and red.

"Hold her tightly, Ephraim, I must set the bone."

Ephraim wrapped his arms around Mary's shoul- ders and Martha held Mary's good leg firmly. Anna grasped the injured leg and gave a quick pull. Martha felt she heard the bone lock into place. Mary screamed in pain and then lay still.

"Mary!" Martha turned to Anna. "Is she dead?"

"No, child, the pain was just too much for her. Her leg must now heal on its own." She turned to Adah. "Do you have a couple of straight sticks?"

Adah hurried to find something and came back with two pieces of narrow wood.

Anna worked quickly splinting the leg so it would stay straight. She turned to Martha. "I will give you some herbs to put in boiling water. It will help her to sleep and ease the pain." She reached in her bag and produced two packets of herbs.

"Thank you for your help, Anna." Ephraim reached into his sash and produced a couple of coins which he gave to her. She nodded her thanks and picked up her bag. She had done all she could.

Ephraim gathered the limp form of his daughter and carried her home. Martha washed the pale, dirty face, streaked with tears, as Mary slept on.

Ephraim stood looking down at his youngest child, then turned to Martha. "I must return to the fields, daughter. Stay with Mary, she will need you in the long hours ahead."

"Yes, Abba. I will have your meal ready when you and Lazarus return."

Ephraim nodded and, with a last sad look at Mary, walked slowly out of the courtyard.

Martha looked down at her sister and shook her head. She had so much to do and now an injured sister to take care of. Mary would be no help to her for a while. She went to prepare some chicken broth.

When Mary awoke, Martha explained to her what had happened. She helped Mary drink a little bit of the chicken broth and patiently persuaded her to take some of the herbal liquid Anna had mixed that would make her sleep.

When Lazarus and her father returned from the fields, dirty and weary, both were eager to see how Mary was doing. Mary still slept soundly. They looked down on her still form, and Lazarus shook his head. "How could Adah let this happen? She is an old woman, perhaps too old to watch children."

"Enough, my son, it has happened and blaming Adah will not undo the damage. We must not speak bitterly against a neighbor."

Their meal was eaten in silence, each occupied with their own thoughts. Just as Martha was putting away their food, there was a knock at the gate. Ephraim went to see who it was and found Gera facing him.

"Bless all within this house. May I speak with you, Ephraim?"

"You are welcome, my friend. Enter our humble home."

Gera stepped into the courtyard just inside the gate.

Martha could barely contain her excitement as she and Lazarus quietly slipped into the house. Though she was anxious to hear what they would talk about, it was not proper for her to be part of the discussion. She stood behind the door, straining to hear Gera's words. Lazarus started to say something and she quieted him with a sharp look. He shrugged and made a face.

The two male voices murmured together for a few moments and then Martha heard the gate close quietly. She waited and then peeked into the courtyard. Her father stood alone, facing the gate, his head down. Then, he turned slowly and came toward the house.

"Martha."

At the tone of his voice, fear shot through her heart. What had happened?

She came and faced her father. "What did he say, Abba?"

"Well, daughter, he thanked me for my kind offer, and was honored that we would consider his son, but it seems they have chosen another maiden for their son's bride."

Martha caught her breath. "Did he say who

31

they have chosen, Abba?"

He sighed heavily. "It is Leah, daughter of Zebulon."

She nodded and struggled with the tears that threatened behind her eyes. "I saw them together at the potter's shop, Abba." She sighed. "I knew Phineas liked her."

Her father put a hand on her chin. "Well, that may have influenced his father, but the matter is now settled. I will find another," he paused, "a man worthy of my beautiful daughter."

Martha thought of the events of the day and knew what she must do. She slowly shook her head. "Abba, if I were to marry, who would take care of you and Lazarus and now Mary with her injured leg? I am needed here."

He looked down at her for a long moment, and she saw the sadness in his eyes, but more than that, she saw his love. "There will be someone for you, daughter, one day, there will be someone." He nodded slowly to emphasize his words, then held out his strong arms and let her weep against him.

That night, while the rest of her family slept, Martha lit a small lamp and looked down at Mary's long lashes and beautiful face. Was Mary flawed now? Would her leg heal properly? If she limped, would it deter anyone seeking a bride? With a heavy heart, Martha crept over to the small chest that held her mother's wedding dress. She set the lamp down and, opening the chest slowly, lifted out the dress, admiring the beautiful fringe and beading. She fingered the lovely blue shawl she'd woven to present to her mother-in-law when she became a bride. Then, picking up one of the gold earrings that had been her mother's, watched it shimmer in the lamp-light. She held it against her ear and then, with a sigh, slowly put everything back.

Tears slid down her cheeks and dropped softly on the linen folds of the wedding dress as she quietly laid her dreams inside the chest and closed the lid.

3

Martha put a hand on Esther's shoulder, her heart breaking for her friend. "What will your father do?"

Esther hung her head. "The priest said he must leave the village. He is unclean."

"What will happen to your family?"

"We may stay. My mother will continue to weave wool from our sheep and sell her yarn in the marketplace. The men will help in our fields when it is time for the harvest. My brother Tobias is almost twenty. He says he will still seek an acceptable match for me, but I'm sure news of my father has traveled to other villages." She shook her head. "Who will want the daughter of a leper?"

"You are one of the prettiest girls in Bethany, Esther. There are many who will want you for yourself, I'm sure."

Esther lifted her water jar to her shoulder. "The God Who Sees knows my heart. I am in his hands. My mother weeps when she thinks Tobias and I are asleep." She started to turn away and then looked back at Martha. "I'm sorry about Phineas. I know you liked him. Will your father seek another match?"

Martha shrugged. "My family needs me now and my father is not feeling well lately. I don't know."

"Mary is recovering?"

"Yes, her leg heals. She can move about more freely now."

Esther's eyes pooled with tears as she nodded, then turned as they went their separate ways.

A few days later, Simon's fate was sealed by a priest in Jerusalem.

Martha and her family stood with their neighbors as Esther's father slowly picked up coins and offerings of food that were placed in front of his house. Everyone had contributed something. He put the coins in a small pouch and the food in a leather bag that hung about his broad shoulders. Known by all for his sense of humor and great heart, this day Simon was somber and bent under the sorrow he carried. Overnight, he'd seemingly become an old man. His wife, Judith, stood at the doorway of their home with tears running down her cheeks, her arms around Esther and Tobias. Forbidden under the law to embrace or touch him, their faces mirrored the anguish they felt.

Simon looked around at each of his neighbors. "I thank you all for your kindness. If it is the will of the God Who Heals, may I be cleansed of this living death and return to our village." He took a step toward his family and murmured softly, "And to you."

Ephraim stepped forward. "We will care for your family, Simon. You need not fear for them."

Simon could only nod. He picked up his staff and, with a last look at his loved ones, turned away and walked slowly down the road.

The evening before at supper, Martha had listened when her father explained to Lazarus and Mary that Simon could never again enter the Holy City of Jerusalem, nor stand with his prayer shawl in the Temple. He must become a beggar, crying "unclean" as he passed by. He must wear a cloth over his face as a symbol of his uncleanness.

Now Martha shuddered anew as she recalled the overwhelming horror that had struck the family of her dear friend. Esther had lost not only her father but probably her chance for marriage.

The two friends met at the well daily, and

Esther's eyes were deep pools of sorrow in her beautiful face. Many a young man in the village had glanced her way with interest before her father's illness.

"Now they look the other way as they pass me on the streets," Esther told Martha one day.

Martha shook her head in sympathy. "This will pass in time, I'm sure of it. You are worthy to be anyone's wife. Give them time and their fathers will be calling on your house to seek a bride."

Esther didn't appear to give much credence to Martha's words. "We'll see. I may never marry."

Esther's words proved to be prophetic for, as the weeks went by, no offers were received for her hand. Martha feared her friend might share her own fate as an unmarried woman.

A few months later as they were finishing their evening meal, they were startled by a knock at the gate. Ephraim rose and ushered Esther into the courtyard.

"May peace be upon this household."

"And with you, Esther."

She nodded respectfully to Ephraim and hurried over to Martha. Her eyes were shining and her face alight with excitement as she looked around at them all. She caught Martha by the hand. "Oh, my friend, I have good news."

Martha took her friend's hand. "You have news? Your father?"

Esther shook her head, her voice catching. "We pray every day for God's mercy and that he will be cleansed, but there is no word." She took a deep breath and then looked up at Martha. "I have come to tell you—I am to be betrothed."

Martha stared at her. "Betrothed? To whom?" She had not heard any word in the village and thought quickly of the eligible young men left in Bethany.

"His name is Micah, and he is a distant cousin from Bethlehem. His father came to see Mother and Tobias. Micah is older, almost twenty-eight. His wife died and his father said he grieved for a long time, and did not wish to remarry, but he changed his mind and now they seek a bride for him from our tribe. He did not want anyone from their village."

"How did his wife die?"

"In childbirth. It is so sad. The baby died also. Tobias told me Micah's father is related to my father's brother." She smiled shyly. "Micah's father said that the bride-price Tobias set for me was fair, considering the circumstances."

Martha started to comment but held her tongue. Beautiful inside and out, at sixteen Esther was well worth a fair bride price, in spite of her father. She sat down on a nearby bench. "You will be moving to Bethlehem." It was not a question, for she knew Esther would go to the home of her husband.

Esther sat down beside her and the two women looked at each other. Martha saw reflected in Esther's face the sadness she herself was feeling. They would no longer see each other every day at the village well.

"We will come to Jerusalem for the Passover. We will see each other then," Esther ventured.

That was true. People streamed into Jerusalem from the surrounding areas of Judea to celebrate Passover at the Temple. It was something they could look forward to. Martha gathered her courage. "I am happy for you. Your father's illness has not kept you from becoming a bride." Esther's beauty must have outweighed any qualms the family had concerning her father.

Esther stood. "The betrothal ceremony will be small, but we want you and your family to come."

Martha smiled and nodded. She must not cause her friend sorrow by wearing a sad face. Surely it was a time of rejoicing.

Tobias signed the betrothal document and the wedding was set for the fall after Elul. Micah's father, Jakin, would then be able to travel the twenty miles to Bethany for the wedding and be home again before the coming of the first rains and Rosh Hashanah.

Knowing Esther's mother had little, the neighbors brought gifts of food and wine to the betrothal party so that she would not be embarrassed in front of the groom's parents.

Martha brought date cakes that had been packed in stone crocks, and loaves of fresh bread. Judith was a gracious hostess, and Tobias, now the head of their house, made sure each guest was made welcome. The neighbors truly rejoiced for Esther in her good fortune, but Martha wondered if it was more out of relief. Not one of them had approached Tobias on their son's behalf after Esther's father left the village.

Now she observed Esther's husband-to-be as he and Esther spoke awkwardly—aware of being watched closely by the other guests. Micah was a tall, thin, serious man with a full beard and dark eyes. Martha began to wonder if he ever laughed and her heart became concerned for her friend. Would he be good to her? Then she shrugged. At least Esther would be a bride, and hopefully one day a mother.

"I hope the children look more like Esther," she murmured to herself.

4

The month of Ab with its summer heat arrived and the grapes shimmered on the vine. Like others in their village, Ephraim's vineyard was interspersed with date palms, should the grape harvest prove to be small. It would give them another crop to harvest for the family needs.

The vineyard usually provided enough to make wine for their family, and some years Ephraim was able to sell some of their wine in the market-place. However, most of the proceeds went to pay the taxes. As she became more proficient in her weaving, Martha began to take her cloth into Jerusalem to trade for other needs of the house-hold. She learned to haggle firmly with the merchants, and sometimes when she won an encounter, she would catch a brief smile on the face of the merchant, who admired her bravery.

The grapes were picked and Martha worked hard alongside her sister to fill the baskets they moved down the rows of vines. Some grapes would be spread out on the ground on cloth to dry into raisins. As with other crops, the poor of the village were allowed to pick the grapes left behind on the vines.

The grapes were pressed immediately by people stomping around in the soft pulp in the wine-presses. Martha sent Mary first to the winepress, glad that her leg had healed well—there was now no sign Mary had been injured. Pressing the grapes was messy, but Mary and Lazarus laughed and teased each other about their red feet as they took their turn pressing the grapes. Their tunics, though tucked up in their girdles, were stained at the end of the day.

Martha, bringing another basket of grapes, smiled at their happy faces and watched the juice run down into the bedrock vat. The juice, after the vat was sealed, remained for a short time until the yeast in the grapes turned the sugars into alcohol. Then her family would work together as they drew the juice into jugs, where it was left to settle for another month or so. Finally, her father would strain the wine to remove any sediment, and it would be stored in large jugs and sealed with beeswax.

When Martha and Esther, taking their turn, pressed the grapes with their feet in the vats, their talk was of the wedding. Esther would wear her mother's bridal dress, but Tobias would purchase new sandals for her. She would need them on the journey to Bethlehem.

One Sabbath afternoon, not long after the grape harvest, Martha and Esther sat under the shade of an ancient olive tree. Esther's wedding was approaching in a few weeks.

Martha glanced at her friend. "Are you fearful of being a bride?"

Esther twisted a blade of grass in her fingers and nodded slowly. "I have wondered how it is between a man and a woman on their wedding night. My mother says she will tell me about this when it is time for the wedding. Tobias said Micah is a kind man and I must do all I can to be a good wife."

Martha hung her head. "At least you will be a bride, Esther. I have this feeling that I shall never marry."

"You are very brave, dear friend. You have a household to take care of, but if God looks with favor on you, perhaps there shall yet be someone."

Martha shrugged. "Perhaps, one day."

They sat in silence for a while and listened to the birds calling to one another among the olive trees.

Martha glanced at her friend. "Have you had word of your father?"

"No," Esther said softly and large tears slipped down her cheeks. "He will not know I am to be a bride. He shall never see my wedding, or bounce grandchildren on his knees."

"I also pray that God will have mercy on him. That he will be cleansed and returned to you one day."

Esther wiped her cheeks with one hand and nodded slowly. "May the God Who Sees be merciful."

Martha was suddenly aware the shadows were lengthening as the sun began its descent behind the mountains. It was nearly time to close the Sabbath. The two friends rose and walked slowly down the dusty road toward the village. As they came to the place of parting, Esther reached out and suddenly embraced Martha. "I will miss having such a friend."

Tears sprang to Martha's eyes and she nodded.

She watched Esther walk away and her heart was heavy.

As Esther's wedding day dawned, Martha opened the small chest and lifted out the deep blue shawl she'd woven to give to a future mother-in-law when she was betrothed. She smoothed the soft material with her hand, then carefully folded it over her arm and joined her family as they walked to Esther's home.

Music came from the small courtyard. A young man in the village played his flute and some of the women the tambourine and small cymbals. The sound lifted Martha's spirits. This was a day for happiness. She would not be sad to mar her friend's wedding day.

Esther's mother, Judith, had made places for the pallets of the groom and his parents who had arrived the evening before, and now she was putting them away in the storage room for the day.

Esther came to the gate to welcome them and Martha held out the shawl. "It is my wedding gift to you. When you wear it, you must think of me and know that I will remember you also."

Esther took the shawl and her eyes were moist. "I will treasure it always."

The two young women entered Esther's home to prepare her for the simple wedding.

Tobias had arranged for four young men to hold the huppah, the canopy brought from Jerusalem by Abijah, the rabbi who taught the young boys in the village. He would also perform the ceremony.

Martha brushed Esther's long hair until it shone. It would be the one day she would wear it down her back. Then Martha, Mary, and Judith helped Esther into her wedding dress and arranged the bridal veil over her headband of coins. She slipped her feet into the new sandals Tobias had given her and was pronounced ready.

Micah was standing in a corner of the courtyard with his parents. As Martha observed him, his eyes darted back and forth, watching the festivities. He didn't smile, and Martha felt a stab of concern for Esther. Was Micah nervous? Perhaps because there was no place for him to gather friends as he would in his own village. He had no friends here. Her tender heart went out to him, and when she caught his eye, she gave him what she hoped was an encouraging smile.

The canopy was held in place and Micah moved into position under it as Tobias proudly led Esther into the courtyard. Walking in a slow circle around the huppah, with his sister on his arm, Tobias stood tall as, in the place of his father, he entrusted Esther to her new husband.

Neighbors and friends joined in the music and dancing and brought what they could spare as gifts. A couple of chickens, bread, pillows stuffed with feathers, wine, and date cakes. Martha was glad the young couple would stay there for their wedding night and leave with Micah's parents for Bethlehem in the morning. With the warmth of the late summer, a pallet had been made on the roof of the house for the bride and groom, decorated with flowers and greenery. It was the most privacy the small house and courtyard could offer.

Esther blushed and Martha pretended not to hear the ribald comments that the men called out to Micah as the newly married couple was ushered to the foot of the stairs leading to the roof of the house. Micah waited while Esther's attendants prepared her for her marriage bed.

Laughing among themselves, the men gathered in the courtyard as their wives began to put away the food. Nathan joined them, but was his usual quiet self. His wife, Rhoda, did not attend. The wasting illness consumed her strength and body, and now she was unable to leave her bed. The village women shook their heads. It was only a matter of time before Nathan was a widower.

Martha and Judith helped remove Esther's wedding dress and Mary carefully lifted off the veil. Martha placed the headdress of coins in a pouch as Esther's dowry, which she was to take with her.

Judith hugged her daughter tightly. "May you be blessed on this day, my daughter, and may your marriage produce fine sons."

Martha hugged Esther also, seeing the fear in her eyes, but words would not come. They had all been spoken before. She could only smile encouragingly at her friend and turn to leave with Judith and Mary. They passed Micah on the stairs. He gave them a brief smile and went slowly up to join his bride.

As the guests left the courtyard to return to their homes, Lazarus walked on one side of his father with Nathan on the other. Ephraim seemed so frail lately and sometimes stumbled.

That night Martha lay awake a long time thinking of Esther and Micah. She knew Esther would be found to be a virgin and hoped Micah was gentle with her. Thinking of marriage, a great longing rose like a wave in her body, and she clasped her hands to her breast to stifle it. Had she cried out? She looked over at Mary and Lazarus and they did not stir. She must put the thoughts of marriage aside now. Chiding herself for her foolishness, she pulled the rug tighter around her body and closed her eyes for sleep.

In the cool of the early morning, Martha woke and lay quietly thinking of the events of the day before. Were all young brides afraid as they awaited the unknown prospect before them? How had it gone with Esther? She rose and dressed quickly, anxious to talk to her friend, but knowing she must prepare a meal for her family. She sliced some bread from the day before, put out some figs and cheese and a pitcher of goat's milk. As Mary, Lazarus, and Ephraim gathered at the table, she made sure they had everything they needed and then hurried out the gate, almost running to Esther's home.

The sun was already spreading its warmth over the village, and she knew the sooner the wedding party was on the road to Bethlehem, the better. Would her friend have a few minutes to talk? Martha's sandals made a soft, slapping sound in the dust as she walked quickly to Esther's home.

To her dismay, Micah and his father were already packing the donkey as Judith helped Esther carry her bundles of wedding gifts and clothes from the house.

Questions ran rampant through Martha's mind, but she could see there was no time to ask them. Then Esther pulled Martha into the courtyard away from anyone who could hear them.

Martha looked into her friend's face and saw happiness. "It went well?"

Esther blushed and whispered, "I think Micah will be a good husband."

The two young women embraced a last time.

"May God be with you, Esther, and give you sons."

"Thank you, dear friend, and may the God Who Sees bless you as you care for your family."

The donkey was soon ready. Esther embraced her mother, brother, and sister-in-law with tears. Martha's family joined her along with a few of the neighbors to see them off.

Martha watched the group move slowly down

the road and felt as if she could not breathe for the weight of the sorrow she carried. Ephraim started to speak to her, but when she turned to him, tears spilling from her eyes, he merely nodded and turned away. She watched until the wedding party became mere specks and disappeared around a bend in the road. Finally she too turned toward her home. The day was beginning and there was work to do.

5

Martha stood in the center of the courtyard of their home in Bethany and watched a hawk circle lazily over the barley fields. The heavy rains of the month of Tebet had stopped and the fields were golden in the warm Judean sunshine. Larks and doves filled the air with their songs as they called to one another. The years like leaves had drifted by, from green and promising spring, to the subtle shades of autumn and winter. Other girls and young men of Bethany had married and had children. As she passed them in the village, she was aware that some of her former friends looked at her with puzzlement and pity. She was nearly twenty, and still unmarried.

She shaded her eyes as she looked up and for a moment envied the hawk as it soared freely on the wind currents. How long had it been since she had done as she pleased? There seemed so much to do and so little time. For a brief moment, tears threatened, and she forced them back. She shook herself as if to dispel the dark thoughts that seemed to occupy her mind lately.

Martha turned toward the road that wound from the village past their home. She was suddenly aware of voices raised in song and intermittent laughter. A group of women were coming down the road. She recognized Phoebe in the middle of the group, and remembered her talking at the well about going to Jerusalem to buy her wedding clothes. The women waved to Martha as they passed but didn't invite her to join them. She waved back as casually as she could, but a great lump had formed in her chest. Phineas. The thought of him and that bitter disappointment still was a wound in her heart, but there was nothing to be done for it. She turned resolutely into their small courtyard.

The smell of fresh bread baking in the outdoor clay oven brought her mind back to the tasks at hand. She put down the basket of leeks and garlic she'd gathered from the outside garden and lifted the bread out with a flat wooden paddle, setting it to cool.

She looked around the small courtyard in front of their humble home and felt a sense of pride. Only slightly larger than most of the humble dwellings in Bethany, their home was made even more spacious by the extensive courtyard Ephraim had built. In a protected area by the side of the house, their three goats butted each other playfully. Next to them their small flock of sheep eyed Martha with their large, soft eyes. The donkey swished his tail and looked up at her expectantly. The animals were hungry, but she turned away. Lazarus would tend to them when he got home.

She moved to the small alcove off the courtyard that served as a storage room for food and cooking pots. Her father had built a covered walkway from the house to the alcove to allow access to the storage room in inclement weather. Martha lifted the leather curtain aside and entered. She put the extra garlic in a small basket, then took a wooden bowl off the shelf for the lentil stew. Her father and Lazarus would be coming back from Jerusalem soon and would want their dinner. She hoped they had been successful in selling her last two weavings. Working the loom was her solace and she loved to mix the rich colors and patterns. When she was old enough to move the shuttle back and forth, her mother had taught her how to weave and showed her the different dyes that could be made from plants and roots. Together they carefully colored the wool yarn Martha had spun. Even at the age of five, she could twirl the spindle expertly, pulling the soft wool into thread.

Now her woven cloth and rugs helped with their income. Brick work had been slow and the crops had not been as bountiful this year.

Emerging from the storage room, she looked around in exasperation. Where was Mary now? At fifteen, Mary was a woman, gentle-natured to be sure, but certainly not very practical, to Martha's way of thinking. Mischief seemed to follow her around, just as it did for Lazarus. Martha sighed with annoyance and shook her head.

Whenever there was work to be done, Mary was often sitting somewhere playing the lyre Lazarus had made for her years before. While Martha blustered at her at times, the music was soothing. Martha had promised her mother to care for her sister, to watch over her and teach her the things of the household. Yet Mary was a tenderhearted dreamer and often left her tasks to care for an injured bird or animal. Martha would choke back her stern words and busy herself in her work.

She heard the sound of the gate and turned to greet her father and Lazarus. They were smiling broadly.

"Ah, daughter, you are truly gifted. We sold both rugs in the marketplace and they were glad to have them and will sell any more we bring them. May the God Who Sees reward you for your fine work."

Martha blushed briefly at the praise, then eyed her brother. "Lazarus, the animals need to be fed, and watch the donkey, you know how he kicks."

Lazarus gave her an impish grin. "You do not want to know the news from the city?"

She put her hands on her hips in mock sternness. "There is something that I should know about?"

Ephraim sighed. "As a matter of fact, many things are happening in Jerusalem. The talk is about a man people believe to be a prophet. They call him John the Baptist. He is baptizing people in the Jordan River, admonishing them to repent of their sins and crying that the kingdom of heaven is at hand."

Lazarus broke in. "People say he wears a garment of camel's hair and eats locusts and wild honey."

"Locusts and wild honey? Now who can survive on that?"

Ephraim smiled at her and then looked out toward the fields, his face almost wistful. "He says he is preparing the way for someone, someone who is coming soon."

Lazarus grabbed a handful of dates from the bowl on the table, avoiding Martha's reproving glance. "The whole city is saying that perhaps it is the Messiah."

Martha gasped. "The Messiah? He is telling them to prepare the way for the Messiah?"

Lazarus nodded his head. "From the talk in the marketplace, people have been coming to him by the hundreds to be baptized and repent of their sins."

"Where is he now?"

Ephraim waved a hand. "He moves from place to place. Harim says the last he heard, the Baptist was in Aenon, near Salim."

Martha considered that a moment, then lowering her voice, asked, "And what do the leaders and priests say of him?"

Ephraim shook his head. "That is the amazing thing. It is whispered that the prophet goes up and down the Jordan, and the elders at first only stood and listened, even when he called them a 'brood of vipers.' "

Martha looked from her father to her brother. "I'm surprised the leaders have not arrested him, calling them names like that."

"That is a dangerous thing, sister, but what will get him killed is denouncing Herod for marrying Herodias, his brother's wife." He shook his head. The adulterous relationship was common knowledge throughout Palestine, but one didn't speak of it openly. Herod's spies were everywhere.

Martha put her hand to her mouth. "He dares to say that openly?"

"The talk in Jerusalem is that Herod is afraid of him. The people follow this prophet and he doesn't want to create problems in his district." Ephraim frowned. "Herod is a great sinner, but he will not repent and be baptized by the likes of this John the Baptist."

Lazarus broke in. "Harim said the priests and Levites were sent by the Elders to ask if he was the Christ, or That Prophet, or Elijah, and he said no. When they pressed him to tell them who he was so they could give an answer to those who had sent them, he would only say, 'I am the voice of one crying in the wilderness; make straight the way of the Lord.' "

Martha shook her head in amazement. "Those are strange words, Abba, and these are strange times. Have there not been many over the years who have claimed to be the Messiah? They gathered followers like this man, but soon they seemed to disappear and that was the end of them."

"True, daughter, but this fellow does not claim to be the Christ. If he is just demented, he will soon lose the interest of the people and they will desert him."

Then a thought occurred to her. "Did you go to be baptized?"

Lazarus grinned at her. "We didn't have time for such things. We had merchandise to sell and a long walk home."

Relieved, Martha returned to her preparations for the evening meal and laid cushions down around the low wooden table.

Lazarus, almost seventeen, had grown into his long arms and legs. He was a handsome young man. The young girls of the village eyed him shyly behind their shawls. He was not yet interested in marriage, and Martha was glad her father was not in any hurry to add to their household.

The gate opened again and Mary stepped into the courtyard.

"Where have you been? Supper is almost ready and you have been no help." The words were out before Martha thought.

Mary hung her head. "Do not be angry with me, sister. Phoebe's goat had triplets. I wanted to see them."

Martha gave an exasperated sigh. Staying angry with her gentle sister was a futile effort. "Come, let us eat."

As they dipped the still warm bread into the lentil stew, Ephraim turned to Martha. "In all this talk about this John the Baptist, I almost forgot. I have heard news of Esther's father, Simon."

She gasped. "Oh Abba, I thought by now he would have died."

"He lives still, the leprosy grows slowly."

"His family will be glad to get any word of him, Abba."

"Yes, I'm sure you are right. It seems a merchant passed him on the road and had pity when Simon called out to him. The merchant was on his way to Jerusalem and would leave a message for his family with Jacob the tanner, to tell them he was still alive."

Martha thought of her friend Esther and her eyes filled with tears. "Does his family know now?"

Ephraim sighed. "Yes. By now they do. For whatever comfort it may bring them."

6

Martha moved her shuttle along the warping stick on the loom and then pushed down to tighten the fabric. Her latest project, another shawl, was nearly finished. This was a plain head shawl to replace the one Mary had torn on a thornbush. She had left the yarn in its natural state, but couldn't resist a contrasting occasional thread of deep green, knowing it was Mary's favorite color.

She listened to her sister play her lyre and found the music soothing. She had not learned an instrument herself. There was no time over the years with the household to see to.

Word came to the village that the Baptist was still baptizing after almost a year and no soldiers had come to arrest him. His words ran through her mind many times over the months: "Prepare ye the way of the Lord." The Lord was coming? The Messiah? She shrugged to herself. The Messiah had been foretold for hundreds of years, since Father Abraham. His people had cried out for him for a long time, but he hadn't come. Would now be any different? Would he suddenly appear and deliver them from their Roman oppressors?

She sniffed. Who was this strange man in the desert? Had God truly sent him? She was only a woman, but through her father she knew of the whispered discussions among the men of her village. They were expectant, hoping against hope that the Messiah would come in their lifetime.

She looked over at Lazarus as he fed the animals. To the amazement of her family, he had asked his father to arrange a betrothal to Shua, the daughter of the village potter. Esther's brother, Tobias, had married the year before. He and his young wife, Chloe, seemed to be very happy together. Perhaps it had influenced Lazarus.

Martha stood to stretch her back. Shua was the only survivor of four children her mother had borne, and her parents doted on her. She was pretty, but a flighty young woman, and Martha had misgivings about her household abilities.

During this year of betrothal, Lazarus had helped his father add another room to their home for his bride. That morning, Martha listened wistfully to her brother singing happily as he worked. She was glad for him, but the thought that marriage might never be her lot brought sadness and a small twinge of jealousy. With effort, she had willed the negative thoughts away and turned her attention to shaping the dough into loaves for the oven.

As she listened to Mary's song, she wondered when Mary would be a bride. Men gazed at her slender figure and her lovely face with interest, but her father insisted she was too young for marriage as yet. Martha shook her head. Mary was almost fifteen, more than eligible for marriage.

Martha eyed her weaving, deciding what colors to add, but her mind returned to Shua. She would have to be trained when she came to their home as a new bride. Martha paused, reflecting. What would it be like having someone else in their household? In some homes in their village, Martha knew there were difficulties. She must do her best to make Shua feel comfortable here, at least for Lazarus's sake.

"Mary, would you bring me some garlic from the garden? Pick some of the young fava beans also."

Mary smiled and rose from her bench. Laying the lyre down, she walked quickly to the gate.

A few minutes later, Martha looked up as Mary came back carrying the garlic and fava beans in a small basket on her arm. Martha's thoughts went back to the day she herself brought leeks and garlic to her mother, the day before Mary was born. Time seemed to be rushing past with the speed of a hawk diving for its prey.

Heavy coughing in the house interrupted her thoughts. At midmorning, Lazarus had helped his father to his pallet, for Ephraim almost fainted while they were weaving the branches over the new room. Her father's health had seemed to improve for a few years, but now it grew worse.

He had little energy and sometimes great pain in his side. Passover neared and both Martha and Lazarus worried he would not be able to make even the short journey to Jerusalem. They had a new donkey, purchased with the money Martha had gotten from the last batch of rugs sold in the marketplace. The donkey they'd had for years had gotten too cranky and began to nip, so they sold him. Her father would have a strong, young animal to ride on, for he was in no condition to walk this year.

Pouring some broth into a cup, she hurried into the house and knelt down by her father's pallet. "Take some nourishment, Abba, it will make you feel better." She put an arm behind his shoulders and lifted him up slightly, putting the cup to his lips. He struggled to drink what he could, and finally she eased him down again.

"Thank you, daughter, I'm sure I can rest now."

He closed his eyes, and for a brief moment a bolt of fear went through her as she remembered her mother's death. Then she watched for his chest to move in rhythm with his breath. She put a fist to her mouth to stifle a sob and rose quickly to leave the room. She needed her father's strength. He must get well. She squared her shoulders. Tomorrow she would go to see Anna. With all her herbs and potions, surely there was something she could do for her father.

• • •

The barley harvest drew to an end and the village prepared for Passover. With Ephraim so weak, Martha asked Lazarus to inspect their three lambs for blemishes and choose the best lamb for the sacrifice in the Temple. Simon's family, now with Tobias's young wife, Chloe, could not afford a lamb, and Martha's family would share the sacrifice as it was allowed in the law of Moses. Along with the lamb, Lazarus and the other families of Bethany took the half-shekel they had carefully saved and placed it in girdles for the Temple treasury.

The sense of joy and excitement increased among the people as strangers began to pass through Bethany on their way to Jerusalem. Martha drew water from the village well and watched as people streamed toward the Holy City from all over Israel to obey the commandment of the Lord. She also watched the groups of travelers in hopes of seeing her friend Esther and her husband coming with his family, but so far there had been no sign of them.

Martha prepared food to be packed on their donkey behind her father and carried to Jerusalem. She was grateful that Hanniel, an elderly cousin on her mother's side, lived in the city and opened his home to the family for lodging during Passover. There they would all partake of the sacrificial lamb after it had been roasted. Not a home, an inn, or a courtyard went unfilled as the pilgrims flooded the city to capacity.

At last the time came to leave for Jerusalem. Lazarus, who was stronger than his sisters, helped their father walk through the courtyard. Mary untied the lamb from the gate of the pen and led it toward the gate. She would also help carry date cakes, flour, and other ingredients for the Passover meal Martha had put together. Mary had carefully put her share of the load into the cloth bag Martha had made to go over her shoulder.

Lazarus helped their father up on their donkey and, at Ephraim's sharp intake of breath, glanced anxiously at Martha. Ephraim was obviously in pain, but resisted their pleas to remain at home. They had no choice but to continue to Jerusalem.

When they were ready to leave, Nathan quietly joined the group. He walked stoically near the donkey and kept a firm eye on Ephraim. Somehow his strong presence made Martha feel less burdened for her father. As they set out, neighbors and friends joined them and the atmosphere of joy was contagious.

She'd been awed as a child by the crowds and the ceremonies of Passover—so much needed to be done by their leaders beforehand. The priests and Levites prepared months ahead. She remembered all that their father had carefully shared with them when they were small. On the first day of Adar, which was a full six weeks before Pass-over, special envoys of the rabbinical court checked over all of the roads, marking gravesites so no one would inadvertently step on one and thus be ritually impure. After the rains of Tebet, some roads needed repair. The city squares and public areas would be cleared so way stations could be set up for pilgrims to spend the night and gather fresh supplies as they journeyed toward the city. Wells, called *mikvaot*, would be prepared along the way where pilgrims would immerse themselves and be purified for the Temple. Ephraim pointed out the special ovens they would see in Jerusalem that were set up all over the city for roasting the lambs.

How gently he led us and explained things to us, Martha mused. She thought of all her father's teaching over the years. How strong he had seemed to her, and now as she watched him, hunched over the donkey, she realized once again how old he had gotten, and how frail.

The group walked steadily, other travelers joining them until a throng flowed toward the Holy City. Martha glanced back at Judith, Tobias, and Chloe. Would their cousin Hanniel object to Simon's family coming into his court-yard to share the roasted lamb? They did not have the disease that tore Simon from them, yet they were his family. She began to pray silently as she walked, for her father, for Simon's family, and for Simon. At this joyous time of the year, she wondered where he was. He had loved Passover and now was forever excluded from the Holy City.

Their neighbor Shaul and his family walked behind Nathan, who came alone due to his wife's illness. As they approached the city, the great crowd of pilgrims swelled in numbers, and Martha glanced back to see Mary's face alight with wonder. Her sister was easily distracted, and could possibly lag behind among the travelers. With a sigh, Martha touched Mary's shoulder and gave her a significant look.

The donkey plodded along and Ephraim was bent over, dozing from time to time. With Nathan on one side of the donkey and Lazarus on the other, they would make sure he didn't fall off. As they approached the city itself, the family stopped at a *mikvaot* for water purification before entering the city. Lazarus and Tobias immersed themselves as the representatives of their family to attend to the sacrifice in the Temple. The others would remain at the home of Hanniel. When each of the families traveling with them were ready, they began the ascent into Jerusalem.

As the huge crowds and the bleating animals entered the city, it seemed to throb with life and energy. Like a mother bird gathering her fledglings under her wings, so Jerusalem gathered her people for the holiest of days.

7

"Mother, Martha!"

Martha turned quickly to see Esther and her husband, Micah, stepping out of the large throng and moving toward them. Esther embraced her mother and then Martha, and everyone began to talk at once. Martha looked at Esther's rounded stomach and smiled broadly. Esther was obviously with child.

Judith beamed at her daughter. "I shall be a grandmother at last. May God be praised." She studied her daughter's face. "You are well? There are no problems?"

Esther laughed and then said, "Only with this husband of mine who will hardly let me out of his sight. You'd think I was a pottery vessel that would break."

Micah's face reddened. "I only wish her to be safe."

Martha, remembering the loss of Micah's first wife and child, turned reproachful eyes on her friend. "Perhaps he has reason, Esther."

Esther's face lit with understanding. She put a hand on her husband's arm and looked up at him, her eyes warm with affection. "He takes good care of me and I am grateful."

Micah appeared relieved as he looked down at his young wife. It warmed Martha's heart to know her friend had found a husband who would love and cherish her.

Mary, who had been waiting politely near Chloe during these exchanges, now stepped forward, her face anxious. "When is the baby due, Esther?"

"Near the time of date harvest." She laughed. "I do not look forward to being a great cow during the heat of Elul." She turned to Mary. "How is your leg?"

"It has healed well."

Esther smiled at her. "I'm glad to hear that, Mary."

Judith interrupted, taking her daughter's arm protectively. "Was the journey difficult? Did you find safe places to stay?"

"We were fine, Mother. We were safe."

Martha glanced past Micah. "Are your parents here?"

He shook his head. "My father hurt his leg. The journey would be too much for him and my mother stayed to care for him."

Tobias beckoned with one hand. "You must come with us and stay at the home of her mother Jerusha's cousin."

Turning to her mother, Esther smiled. "We wondered if we could find you in the crowd. We went by our home and no one was there."

Her brother shrugged. "We weren't sure when

you were coming or if you were going to be at Passover this year."

She gave him a saucy look. "You could have waited a little longer."

Martha waved a hand. "There is no need to be concerned with that now. We have all found each other and can go together."

Ephraim, waiting patiently on the donkey, nodded his head. "They will be welcome at the home of Hanniel."

Clapping a firm hand on Micah's shoulder, Tobias grinned. "So, brother, you are to be a father. That is good."

Micah winced at the strength of the hand on his shoulder, but smiled weakly. "Yes, that is good."

Lazarus looked around and frowned. "Come, let us get out of this crowd."

The blacksmith stood quietly, watching the reunion with a wistful look in his eyes. He lifted his chin and, with a nod to Ephraim, took his leave of them, disappearing quickly into the mass of people.

Ephraim watched Nathan go with a pensive look on his face. "Perhaps he is also staying with relatives in the city."

Chloe had not uttered a word during the family reunion, and Mary, seeing the girl's shyness, put a gentle hand on her arm. "Come, we have much to do. We will need your help." Chloe smiled then and walked with Mary as the group moved forward.

Hanniel was getting along in years as was his wife, Sherah, but the travelers were greeted warmly and assigned places in the courtyard to bed down and put the supplies they brought.

"You are welcome at this Passover time. Make yourselves comfortable and enjoy our humble home." Sherah made sure Ephraim had a comfortable place to sleep. He thanked her and made his way to a nearby bench, slowly lowering himself. Martha watched him and saw his face, drawn with the effort of the journey. How much longer would he be with them?

Martha presented Sherah with a shawl she'd woven in the soft colors of the earth, a gift in thanks for taking them all in. The older woman fingered the beautiful weaving.

"God has truly blessed you with a gift for this, Martha. This is fine work. It will help keep me warm, for I must confess these days I feel the cold more and more."

As the noon hour approached, when the Temple gates would open, Tobias and Lazarus prepared to bring the sacrificial lamb to the Temple. Ephraim, exhausted from the journey, sat with Hanniel under the shade of a sycamore tree and talked quietly. Martha could hear the panicked animals, perhaps sensing danger, bleating as they were being led to slaughter. Soon the blasts of the Levite trumpets signified the gates to the Temple were closed and the service had begun.

The continual singing of the Levite choir, accompanied by harps, lyres, and cymbals, filled the air. Songs and the Hallel, six songs of praise, resounded throughout the city.

Martha and the other women prepared the oven with pomegranate branches to roast the lamb. As they waited in the courtyard of the house for Tobias and Lazarus to return, Martha took a deep breath, feeling the overwhelming sense of joy that seemed to pervade the city. Listening to the choirs singing in the distance, she could imagine the ceremony taking place at the Temple as her father had described to her. The lambs slaughtered, the blood caught in the silver and gold vessels and then passed on to the priest standing at the altar, who poured the contents on the foundation of the altar.

In time, the smell of roasting lamb in the special ovens filled the city as the women prepared the seder with bitter herbs and matzoth, the bread made without yeast, as Moses had instructed their ancestors long ago.

All at once, the singing from the Temple stopped. Martha looked up. The women exchanged puzzled glances as they became aware of a faint disturbance coming from the Temple. They could hear shouting. Martha's heart pounded. Was it soldiers? Even Herod would not disrupt Passover.

The gate was flung open and Tobias and Lazarus

burst into the courtyard. Tobias carried in the slain sacrificial lamb as Lazarus hastily closed the gate.

The women hurried forward to meet them. Martha looked from one to the other. "What is it? Why has the singing ended?"

Lazarus glanced back toward the Temple, his eyes wide with fear. His father rose and stood unsteadily, his brows knit in concern.

Tobias turned to the group. "The whole Temple is in an uproar. We had just finished our turn at the altar of sacrifice when suddenly there was a commotion in the courtyard. This rabbi no one had seen before was overturning the tables of the moneychangers—"

Then Lazarus broke in. "The Temple police had to force the people back from gathering the scattered coins. Then this rabbi released the pens of Temple lambs, and the doves from their cages. He'd made a whip of cords and drove the moneychangers out of the Temple!"

Tobias shook his head. "We were almost run over by a flock of lambs running every which way. Everything was just chaos. We were walking to the gate when this rabbi burst in. We managed to make our way through the crowd and slip out of the Temple during the uproar. We hurried back here as quickly as we could."

Martha put her hands on her hips. "Who is this new rabbi? What right did he have to do this?"

Tobias was still breathing heavily. Evidently

the two young men had run all the way from the Temple through the narrow streets with Tobias carrying the lamb.

Lazarus took a deep breath. "He was shouting, 'Take these things away! Do not make my Father's house a house of merchandise.' "

Mary's brow was wrinkled in puzzlement. "He said 'my Father's house'? The Temple is the house of God and he called God 'my Father.' Could he be the Messiah we have waited for?"

The men were suddenly silent and stared at her, considering the enormity of her statement. Then Ephraim looked toward the Temple and slowly shook his head. "Many have come over the years claiming to be the Messiah. They have gathered followers, but as time passed they disappeared and their claims came to naught. We will wait to see what this man will do."

Hanniel pounded his fist into his palm. "If he is an imposter, we will know soon enough. I am amazed that the Temple police did not arrest him. Why did they not stop him?" He shook his head. "They have not arrested John the Baptizer either. Are they afraid of these men?"

Martha had been listening, but realized Tobias was still holding the lamb. "This is all very well, but the lamb needs to go into the oven." She motioned to Sherah and Judith, and together they prepared the lamb and sealed it for roasting.

Esther, still weary from the long walk from

Bethlehem, sank down on a bench to rest. Micah hovered nearby, watching her. Her offers to help were declined as the women looked out for her. Now Chloe and Mary sat with her, and the three women whispered among themselves.

As the lamb roasted, Martha nodded to Mary and Chloe to join her as the women put out the food they had prepared. While she worked, Martha's mind was filled with questions. Who was this rabbi? She wished she could have seen him for herself. Would this incident bring the Roman soldiers down on the people? She feared for her family. Would it be safe to travel the road back to Bethany? She glanced at her father, deep in conversation with the other men as they compared the Scriptures referring to the Messiah. She caught snatches of their words . . .

"The Messiah would be born in Bethlehem . . ."

"Does anyone know where this man comes from?"

She heard Tobias's voice. "Nazareth. I heard someone say the rabbi was from Nazareth, as we were pushing through the crowd."

"Then he can't be the Messiah. Nothing good ever came out of Nazareth."

"The Scriptures say he will free our people, he will be a conquering Messiah . . ."

"The leaders did not arrest him. They only questioned why he did this."

She heard Lazarus's voice. "He said, 'Destroy

71

this Temple and in three days I will raise it up.' "

Hanniel gave a hoot of derision. "It took forty-six years to build the Temple. The priests said so. How can he raise it in three days? I say he is demented."

The men continued to argue.

The women waited patiently, talking quietly among themselves and wondering what this all meant. Before they knew it, the lamb was ready and the families gathered around low tables to conduct the seder. The women served the matzoth and bitter herbs dipped in *harose*. Martha loved this dish made from apples and dried fruit, mixed with nuts and wine. As they dipped the matzot in this fragrant dish, Ephraim haltingly told the story of how it represented the mortar used by the Jews to build the pyramids when they were slaves in Egypt.

Hanniel, as host, told the story of the Exodus and finally all ate of the warm meat of the lamb. To the relief of all, they heard the singing resume and the women were assured that meant the Passover ceremonies were continuing. As midnight approached, all three families raised their cups for the singing of the Hallel, the prayers of thanks. The song reverberated throughout the city as families by the thousands joined in from every house and courtyard, drawing to a close the holiest day of the year.

As she prepared her pallet for the night, Martha

whispered to Lazarus, "Do you know who that rabbi was, creating the riot in the Temple?"

Lazarus yawned. "I heard someone call him Jesus." He closed his eyes and in moments was asleep.

Martha lay back, looking up at the night sky. These were strange times and strange things were happening. Would Herod send soldiers because of the riot in the Temple, or would he ignore it and let the Jewish leaders handle it? Would they reach their home safely? She closed her eyes, but her mind reeled with the events of the day, and she wondered what the coming dawn would hold.

8

Martha and the rest of their traveling group prepared for departure. Sherah gave each family some fruit and cheese. Her hand shook as she held out her gifts, and Martha wondered if she would be there to greet them the following year.

Micah and Esther would return to Bethany, then would rest overnight before continuing on to Bethlehem. With Esther's pregnancy and Ephraim's poor health, the group would travel slowly.

Ephraim insisted on walking out of the city on his own and made the laborious descent from the city to the road. By the time he reached the road, he was greatly fatigued and reluctantly allowed Lazarus and Micah to help him on the donkey. Lazarus led the donkey but glanced back every few moments, keeping a close watch on his father.

The group was about halfway to Bethany when there were shouts from the people behind them as a group of Roman soldiers on horseback clattered down on them. People jumped quickly out of the way, but the donkey, sensing danger, balked and Ephraim slipped from the donkey on the side away from Lazarus and fainted in the road, right in the path of the soldiers.

Martha cried out and caught Mary's arm. Micah grabbed Esther against him protectively and turned his back to the road. Tobias pulled Chloe and his mother off the road. Other pilgrims who saw Ephraim fall also cried out. Lazarus tried to get out of the way of the terrified donkey and reach his father before he was trampled, but though he moved quickly, he was not fast enough. Just as Martha was sure her father would be killed, the Roman officer in the lead reined his horse to an abrupt halt and stood his ground in front of the old man so the other soldiers had to ride around him. His quick thinking saved Ephraim's life.

The other soldiers rode on without even a backward glance, but the Roman officer dismounted and stooped to check on the still figure lying in the road.

Lazarus knelt and gathered his father in his arms. He turned to the soldier. "We owe you his life. May you be blessed for your kindness."

The soldier looked at him and smiled. "I am glad to help." His eyes were a deep blue in a rugged face, marked by scars of war. In spite of that, it was a kind face and Martha saw no disdain in the look he gave them.

"I am Captain Flavious, at your service."

Martha's eyes met the eyes of the captain, and in that brief instant, something changed inside her. Bewildered, she lowered her eyes. What was this strangeness she felt?

Lazarus was about to try to place his father on the donkey as Micah and Tobias moved to help. Ephraim was like a dead weight.

The captain shook his head. "I don't believe he will be able to stay on." He lifted the unconscious old man in strong arms and remounted his horse. "Where can I take him?"

Lazarus glanced around at his family and then at Tobias, unsure of what to do. "We are from Bethany." He didn't want to argue with a Roman soldier.

Martha stepped up. "Lazarus, take the donkey and lead Captain Flavious to our home. We will follow as quickly as we can."

Esther put a hand on her arm. "We will come with you."

"Thank you." She covered Esther's hand with

her own briefly and turned away.

As she and Mary walked as fast as they could, Martha's mind was turning. This Roman soldier was a Gentile. Romans were familiar with their kosher ways. Surely he would know he could not enter their home.

Martha and Mary nearly ran to keep up behind Lazarus and Captain Flavious. When they reached the house, panting from their exertion, the soldier was handing Ephraim down to Lazarus. Knowing her father was too heavy for Lazarus to carry by himself, she sought for some solution without involving the soldier entering their house.

"Let me take him."

She turned to face Nathan, who had appeared unexpectedly and was already lifting her father in his strong arms. He gave the captain a brief nod of thanks and dismissal and as Lazarus opened the gate, carried Ephraim to his pallet. Mary hurried into the house behind them, her face pinched with fear.

Martha turned to their benefactor. "You are very kind, Captain Flavious. We owe you a great debt of thanks."

The captain's blue eyes caught hers and something fluttered in her heart. Why was this man affecting her so?

He swung up onto his horse and gave her a brief smile. "Perhaps I will see you again in the city?"

Her thoughts flew. Did he want to see her

again? She wanted to say the right thing, to discourage that thought, but instead murmured only, "Per-haps, Captain."

He seemed pleased. "Will you tell me your name, and those of your family?"

She hesitated. Would something come of this incident with the authorities? He seemed trustworthy and kind. Perhaps there was no harm in telling him the names of the family he had helped. "I am Martha. My father is Ephraim, my brother and sister are Lazarus and Mary."

"I'm happy to make the acquaintance of your family—Martha."

He wheeled his horse and rode quickly out of Bethany, leaving Martha staring after him with mixed emotions. As she turned back toward the house, she nearly ran into Nathan. How long had he been standing in the courtyard? Had he overheard their conversation? His dark eyes were unreadable, but he turned to walk away, his whole demeanor stern with disapproval.

She felt her face redden with shame as she hurried toward her father. She had been open and friendly with a hated Roman soldier. Yet the man had saved her father. The village already knew about the captain's kindness. Would Nathan relate what he had heard to others in the village? He was a taciturn man not given to gossip. She hoped that would be the end of it.

Micah and Esther arrived with her family and

found that Ephraim was safely home being cared for and the Roman soldier was gone. At Martha's insistence, they went home. Martha and Esther agreed to meet early in the morning to have a short visit before Esther and Micah went on their way.

The two young women walked slowly together to the shade of a sycamore tree near Esther's home in the cool of the early morning.

"Marriage agrees with you, Esther. You look beautiful."

"It is a good marriage. He is a kind man as Tobias said. His parents try to give us as much privacy as they can." She blushed. "Many times when the weather is good we sleep on the roof. I am happy in Micah's arms."

Martha smiled and just nodded. "When do you have to leave?"

"Tomorrow. Micah knew I wanted to spend some time with my mother, and we will stay an extra day, but he is concerned for his father and is anxious to return."

"I wish you could stay longer, but it is better. You will have other travelers on the road from Passover and it will be safer for you."

Esther unconsciously rubbed her stomach. "Another month and I don't think I would be able to travel very far. I am so tired most of the time."

"I remember when my mother was carrying

Mary. She was tired all the time too. Perhaps this is just the way of things in the beginning."

"Perhaps." Esther looked toward her home and saw Micah standing in the gateway, looking their way. "I think I am needed." She turned to Martha. "Take care, my friend. There will be a husband for you one day, I know it."

Martha watched Esther move slowly toward Micah and saw how carefully she walked. Micah slipped an arm around his wife and led her into the courtyard. Martha listened to the sparrows chirping and, as she started for home, found she was smiling to herself.

9

Ephraim was weak and stayed on his pallet many days as Martha brought him nourishing soup to give him strength. Lazarus worked in the village on two houses that needed bricks replaced and also spent time in their field. Mary kept watch over her father and played her lyre for him when he asked. Martha went about her chores, but from time to time was distracted by a scarred face with deep blue eyes that seemed to appear in her thoughts at unexpected moments. She chided herself, knowing she must not see him again. He was a Gentile and she kept a kosher home. There was no way their worlds could or should cross.

That Sabbath, Ephraim could not rise from his pallet, and the family moved into his small room as Lazarus led the Sabbath prayers with his father merely nodding his head. Lazarus and Mary went with Nathan to Jerusalem to celebrate the Sabbath, but Martha stayed behind to watch over her father.

When the family returned and Ephraim again slept, Mary offered to stay with him and Martha slipped out to walk to the Mount of Olives. With so many things on her mind, she sought solace for her worries in Gethsemane.

As she sat under a tree, praying for her father, she was aware of someone nearby, hidden by the trees. Her hand went to her mouth as fear gripped her heart. She was alone. Was she in danger? She'd never felt fear in this place before; it had been a sanctuary. But now she realized how foolish she was to be here with no one around to hear her cries should she be assaulted.

She rose quickly, prepared to run for her life, and at that moment a deep voice stopped her.

"Do not be afraid, Martha. It is only me, Captain Flavious. I didn't mean to startle you."

She turned to see him walking quietly toward her. To her surprise, she felt no fear, only a sense of gladness.

"Do you come here often?" His voice was soft now, and gentle.

"Yes, usually on Sabbath afternoons, when I cannot do work at home." She frowned, puzzled. "How did you know I was here?"

He laughed. "To tell you the truth, I didn't. When I was assigned to Jerusalem, I sought a place away from the barracks to think, and pray."

"You pray here to your Roman gods?"

He shook his head. "No, I pray to the one God, Jehovah."

She looked at him closely, wondering if he was telling the truth. "You are a Godfearer?"

"Yes. My mother was Jewish and taught me about him when I was little. My father was Roman, and while he did not believe, he allowed her to speak of those things to me."

He glanced around as did Martha, but the trees hid them from prying eyes.

"Would you like to sit down?" He indicated a grassy knoll.

She shook her head, suddenly self-conscious. "I must go. It is nearly the end of the Sabbath."

"Yes, I see that it is. May I talk with you again sometime?"

Her thoughts flew. She should not see him again, even if he was a Godfearer, but she knew she wanted to. "Perhaps the next Sabbath?"

He studied her face and she felt herself leaning toward him, but caught herself in time.

"Perhaps the next Sabbath," he replied softly.

He strode away through the trees toward

Jerusalem, and she watched his tall figure until he was out of sight. What was she doing? She had told him that she would possibly see him again. She walked quickly toward her home, nodding a greeting to a neighbor on the way. Did the woman look at her strangely? Was she imagining things? Martha pulled her shawl closer around her face.

Ephraim remained on his bed all week, for Anna had done her best, but there was no change in his condition. After an inner struggle, the next Sabbath afternoon, Martha left him in Mary's loving care and announced she needed to take a walk. She ignored the question in Mary's eyes and hurried out the gate. Her heart pounded as she entered the olive grove. Captain Flavious was waiting.

They walked slowly through the trees, and she marveled how at ease she felt with him.

"You are not married." It was a simple statement rather than a question.

"No. How did you know?"

He grinned, looking almost boyish. "I have my sources. You chose to take care of your family."

"How long have you been in the Roman army?"

"Almost twenty years to rise to my present rank. My oldest brother inherited the estate of my father, and it was suggested that my second brother and I join the military. My father was a general, serving in Rome. This is to be my last outpost. I plan to retire to a small villa my father left me in Cyprus."

Too soon their time together was ending. "May I call you Martha? My given name is Thaddeus. I reserve that for . . . friends." He gazed at her earnestly. "Because of my mother, I know your customs. I don't wish to make any trouble for you, but I look forward to another Sabbath and talking with you. You are a very brave woman and have given up much for your family."

He held a small twig between his fingers and broke it as he gazed out toward Bethany. "I was betrothed once. She decided against the life of a soldier's wife and returned to her family."

A shadow crossed her heart. "Are you still betrothed, Thaddeus?"

"No, she broke our betrothal and married another. They have two children. It was for the best. I was away from home more than I was there."

The fact that he was not married caused a small fluttering in her breast. "When will you leave the army?"

"The end of the year." He smiled at her. "At least that was my plan. Now I find a certain woman may cause me to delay." His eyes searched her face. "Could I hope that in spite of our different backgrounds . . ." He took a breath. "From the moment I met you in the road to Bethany, there has been something between us.

I felt it and I know you felt it too. Since my mother is Jewish, I am considered a Jew, but due to the fact my father is Roman and has great standing with the Roman army, I became a soldier, but I had to fight my way up the ranks." He smiled ruefully. "I tell you this for selfish reasons, hoping to persuade you to consider me . . ."

"As a friend?" She interrupted, afraid of what he would say next, yet eager to hear the words.

He smiled then and his eyes searched hers. "Yes, for now. I am not young, Martha. While I do not have a great deal to offer, when I am able to leave the army I shall have a small pension, the villa, and also a monthly stipend from my father. It would be an adequate income for a family to live on . . ."

She looked away toward Jerusalem for a long moment. Then she faced him. "Do you know what that would mean for me?"

He nodded. "To be separated from one's family and possibly ostracized by friends and neighbors, perhaps even family. Yes, I know, but nevertheless, I can hope."

She was never one to hide her feelings. As she gazed at his face, a door opened in her heart. She felt light inside, and for a moment, the obstacles between them seemed as feathers to be brushed away. Then she sighed. Reality was another thing.

She put a hand on his arm. "Let us be friends for now, Thaddeus. I find my mind whirling with many thoughts and I must sort them out. There is something between us, but it has happened so quickly."

He nodded sagely and spoke softly. "I won't rush you. Until next Sabbath . . . Martha."

"Until next Sabbath . . . Thaddeus."

He turned and strode quickly into the trees.

She dawdled on her way home, her mind in turmoil as her heart and her sense of duty warred within her. Would she go to the grove next Sabbath? With a sigh, she knew she would. And what would she say?

"Oh God, have mercy on me and give me wisdom. I don't know what to do." She needed to work; it was her solace. She must keep her thoughts from flying in foolish directions.

The weeks in between Sabbaths seemed an eternity. She hoped the family would put her obvious distraction down to her concern for her father. With Esther gone, there was no one she dared share her secret with, and it burned within her.

That Sabbath, when she reached the olive grove, she looked anxiously about. Then in a moment, Thaddeus was there. Only her strong will kept her from flinging herself into his arms. They sat in a shady spot, careful not to sit too near, for she sensed his longing was as tangible as hers.

"It goes well with you, Martha?"

"It goes well." Where could she begin to voice

what had grown so quickly from bud to flower within her heart? The conversation was mundane. He talked of the army and she of the events in their village. Whenever she happened to glance up and meet his eyes, they drew her into their depths, and with effort, she looked away.

"Martha, my time in Jerusalem draws to a close. I've learned I may be sent back to Rome to prepare for separation from the army. I have a few weeks at most. I would give you time, a year if I could, to think of these things, but I must speak now. I know that in the eyes of your village, you are past the age of marriage . . ."

Her chin lifted. "Do you pity me, Thaddeus?"

"No, my beloved, for that is what you are to me. I see a woman with strength and courage . . . and beauty. I would offer you marriage, and a villa in Cyprus where we could raise a family. As I told you before, I am able to provide for you." He leaned toward her. "I do not want to return there alone."

He thought her beautiful. She was touched beyond words. It was her last chance for marriage and children . . . and he loved her. Still she hesitated.

Her voice was almost a whisper. "You ask at great cost, Thaddeus."

"You would not be mistreated as a Jewess on Cyprus, beloved."

"Your offer brings joy to my heart, but my

father needs me right now. I cannot leave him for this. It would break his heart."

His shoulders sagged as he nodded. "I understand, but I will hope—until they order me to Rome."

She searched his face and realized how dear he was to her. She could not ask him to wait forever.

As if reading her thoughts, he took a step closer. "I will wait a little longer."

They seemed to move toward each other as one, and as his strong arms closed about her, she felt as if she could stay there forever. She laid her head against his shoulder, feeling the strength of his body. He seemed to sigh and, with reluctance, put her away from him. He smiled down at her upturned face and brushed her forehead with a light kiss.

"I would wish more than that, beloved, but for now, let that be a seal between us."

She moved back from him until only the tips of their fingers touched and finally she turned away. She could not look back at him, for she would have run back into his arms and promised anything. She lifted her shawl over her head and walked home as a tear slid slowly down one cheek.

10

The dream had been sweet. She was wrapped in Thaddeus's arms, looking out toward the sea. Someone was calling and she was shaken awake by her sister Mary.

"Martha, come quickly. It is Abba. I don't think he is breathing."

It was barely light, but Martha rose quickly and followed her sister to her father's pallet. Mary had taken to sleeping near her father through the night lest he wake and need her. Lazarus awakened and he too hurried to his father.

Ephraim lay peacefully on his pallet, his face serene in death. He'd left them quietly in his sleep sometime during the night.

Mary began to weep softly and Lazarus remained on his knees, his head bowed over the body of his father. Martha felt hot tears roll down her own cheeks as she tore the part of her tunic over her heart to express her grief. She had leaned on her father's wisdom so long, and now he was gone. First her mother and now her father—the weight of the responsibility felt like a stone in her heart. It was all on her shoulders now.

As soon as it was light, Lazarus went to tell Nathan and the neighbors. Martha sent Mary for

Anna and Helah to begin the *aninut*, the preparation time. When they came, the women prepared Ephraim's body for burial, rubbing it with oil. The women helped Martha lift the body to wrap it in long strips of linen and tucked fragrant spices in the folds. Mary bound his head with a linen napkin. The local rabbi was sent for to say the kaddish, the mourning prayers, for him. Most of the village came out of their homes to join in the funeral procession. The women wept with loud cries, flinging up dust and tearing their clothes as a sign of great mourning. Ephraim's body was borne on a bier through the town to the place of burial and the entrance sealed with a stone. Mary and Martha wept as they left the tomb, but Lazarus walked stoically beside them, his eyes dry but his face a mask of pain.

When they returned to the house, Judith brought eggs, a symbol of life, and bread. It was the *seudat havraah*, the meal of condolences. During the seven days of mourning, the shivah, Martha, Mary, and Lazarus sat on low stools, and the sisters wept together. No clothes were changed, no meals prepared. Their feet were bare as a sign of mourning and no work was done in any way. For Martha, whose life revolved around her household, it did not matter. The burden of responsibility for her family was like a great cloak that had been laid on her shoulders. Food was brought by friends and neighbors. Martha watched her brother as he sat, unshaven, staring at the floor. If only he would give vent to his grief. He recited the kaddish each day as required by a son for his father, standing up before the minyan of ten men, affirming according to the law, the merit of his deceased father, but otherwise said little. Martha knew he would recite the kaddish each day of the eleven months of the *avelut*, the period prescribed for mourning a parent.

"Lazarus." She touched him on the shoulder. "What can I do for you?"

He gave her a wan smile and shook his head. "Do not fear for me, sister, I will be all right."

Nathan came after the seven days of shivah, and the two men left the courtyard to walk in the fields and talk. Martha watched them go and felt somewhat comforted. Nathan was a friend and loved their father. Perhaps Lazarus could unburden himself with Nathan.

Lazarus returned some time later and his countenance had lifted. She could see by his face that he had wept. He had vented his grief at last.

At the end of the thirty days of mourning, Martha watched Lazarus as he went down the road to return to his jobs in the village. Martha knew her authority must decrease as Lazarus took his place as head of the household. With a deep sigh, she went to her loom to finish a cloth she'd started before her father died. As she sent the shuttle along the strands of wool, her mind remained on Lazarus.

She had been like a mother to him for so long that she'd always seen him as a boy. Yet now it was as if an invisible hand gripped her heart. Was this how every mother felt when suddenly she sees that the child she's nurtured is no longer a child? This morning it was not a boy who looked back at her, but a man.

Mary went about her work, but her mood was somber, and when she had the opportunity, she poured out her sorrow in the minor keys of the songs she played on her lyre.

Martha was not able to go to the Mount of Olives for the month of mourning, and she wondered if Thaddeus knew about her father. The next Sabbath, in the quiet of the afternoon, she felt free to once again go to the Garden of Gethsemane. She told Mary she just needed to go for a walk and hated herself for her deceit. Fortunately Mary had other things on her mind and nodded absentmindedly. Lazarus was away, visiting with Shua.

Ignoring the guilt that followed like a shadow, Martha walked quickly to the grove of olive trees, praying Thaddeus would be there. When he stepped from among the trees and held out his arms, this time she ran into them gladly.

"I heard about your father," he said gently as he held her. "I'm so sorry. I would have come to you, but that would have caused more harm than good and I would not cause you more pain."

She looked up at him through her tears. "I knew you couldn't come. I understand."

"How is it with your household? Your brother and sister?"

They walked slowly together through the grove.

"Lazarus keeps his grief to himself and will not talk about it. Mary weeps silently and plays her lyre. The melodies are sad, and hard for me to hear, but I could not ask her to stop. I miss my father greatly. Ill as he was, he gave me strength."

"Martha, I would be happy to make a home for your brother and sister also if they would let me. They would be welcome."

Her heart swelled with love for him, but she shook her head. "Lazarus is to be married. He won't leave our home, for it will be his and Shua's if I leave. As to Mary, that will have to be her decision. I'm sure she will wish to marry and remain in the village." She shook her head. "Oh, Thaddeus, my heart tells me to go with you, but I just don't know what to do."

He turned and drew her close again, drawing a rough finger slowly down her cheek. He would not shame her by trying to kiss her, knowing Jewish customs, but he looked at her face intently.

"I am going on patrol with my men tomorrow. We have word where we can find a robber and murderer by the name of Barabbas, and we are to hunt him down and capture him. I don't know how long I will be gone, beloved, but can I hope for your answer when I return?"

She nodded wordlessly and laid her head against his broad chest with a small sigh of contentment. She was loved by a decent man who could offer her marriage, to take away the shame of her spinsterhood. And he wanted children. She could be a mother at last. Her heart fluttered in her chest.

He gently put her away from him. "You tempt me, beloved, but I cannot treat you as a street woman. When we come together, it will be as man and wife." He touched her cheek again. "Until I return . . ."

"Until you return," she whispered as he left her standing forlornly among the trees.

Walking back, she alternated between euphoria and panic. Her heart was saying yes and her mind gave all the practical reasons why it would not work. How could she abandon her home and all she'd known? Would Mary somehow elect to go with her or stay with Lazarus? Also, Lazarus was about to be married. Shua was a sweet girl, but she was young. How could she take over the responsibilities of their household?

Martha slipped quietly through the gate and closed it behind her. She quickly began to put together their supper, avoiding Mary's eyes. Guilt filled her heart and in her frustration she snapped at her sister.

"Mary, must you move so slowly? Bring the platters for the table."

At the sharp tone of voice, Mary gave her a questioning look, but said nothing. Martha was instantly contrite. She alternated between clattering the cooking pots to long moments staring off into space. More than once she caught Mary looking at her with raised eyebrows. From time to time she also caught Lazarus watching her, his brows knit in concern. She missed his cheerful attitude and would almost welcome one of his pranks, but he was silent.

Even Nathan, who did not come to the house as often as he had done when Ephraim lived, passed her in the village with a look of pity on his face. Did he suspect something? Had she been seen with Thaddeus? In her anxiety to meet him, had she been careless and not watched to see if anyone from their village was near?

Her questions were answered one night when Mary was asleep. Lazarus came to her out in the courtyard as she sat looking up at the stars.

"They will not give you the answer you seek, Martha."

She turned, startled. "What do you mean?"

He sat down beside her. "You are my sister and I love you. It is my duty to protect you, even from yourself." His eyes flashed. "It is known that you are meeting a Roman soldier in the olive grove."

Her heart thudded in her chest. "The village knows?"

He shook his head. "I thought you were acting strangely and followed you this last Sabbath. When I saw who you were meeting, I was afraid for you." He folded his arms. "Nathan also knows. I wanted to talk to someone. I didn't know what to do."

She gasped. "How could you share this, with Nathan of all people?"

"He is a friend. Who else can I speak of this with? Someone needed to stop this dangerous liaison. Martha—a Roman soldier, how could you shame our family in this way?"

It was the first time Lazarus's anger had been directed at her and she was taken back.

"Actually, you were not as careful as you thought. Nathan already knew."

Nathan knew. Who else knew? Was she now the topic of village gossip? Martha felt her face flame.

"Nathan was on his way back from the city and saw you running into the grove. He thought there was something wrong and was concerned for you. He followed to see if he could be of help. Unfortunately he saw you with the captain. We have kept it to ourselves, hoping you would come to your senses."

He flung his hands in the air. "You must end this, Martha. I have never known you to be so foolish. Tell me, has anything happened between you?"

She knew what he was asking. "No, he has been respectful, Lazarus, and kind. We only talk." She blushed in the darkness, thinking of the last time when she had shamelessly leaned on Thaddeus's chest.

She sighed deeply. In a way she was glad Lazarus knew. She had desperately wanted to talk with him about it. Nathan was another matter.

Lazarus took her by the shoulders. "You must stop this foolishness now, Martha. It is wrong and you know it. What will happen to your reputation should anyone else find out?"

She hated the pleading note in her words. "Lazarus, he has asked me to marry him. He has a villa on the island of Cyprus and can offer me a home . . . and children. His mother was Jewish and he is a Godfearer. We would raise our children in our faith."

Surely Lazarus understood what that meant to her. He was silent, dropping his hands to his sides. She held her breath, waiting for his response.

"You would leave your family and village behind?"

"Oh, Lazarus, I am so torn. I love him." She began to weep, wiping her eyes with her sleeve.

It was the first time Lazarus had seen her so vulnerable, and knowing what he could have said, she was surprised at his next words.

"You have given up much to care for Mary and me, to tend the home for our father. I think I can see how this would happen. I know you want to be married and there is no hope for that in our village for you now." He paused, choosing his words. "You are a good woman, Martha, and a good sister. You must do what you feel is right." He sighed. "While I do not approve of this relationship, I will not renounce you as my sister for your choice."

"Thank you for your kind words, Lazarus. It is more than I hoped for."

He shook his head. "I cannot think that this will be what you want it to be. Have you told him you would go with him?"

"No. He had to leave on a mission and I promised him an answer when he returns."

He stood. "I see. Then I pray that you will bring him the answer that is right—for both of you." He turned and, shaking his head, went to his pallet.

Martha stood in the moonlight for a long time, praying, and finally she too walked toward the house. She lay down wearily on her pallet and stared at the ceiling. How could she bring sorrow on her family? At least her father was gone now; she couldn't have borne his disappointment in her. She frowned. How many times had Nathan seen her when she thought no one was watching? How many times had he followed her? She knew with certainty that she was not going to stop meeting Thaddeus, but she must be more careful—especially when she knew who to watch for.

11

Nathan's wife, Rhoda, was dead. She finally succumbed after years of struggling with an unexplained illness. Unlike the family of Ephraim, Nathan buried his wife quietly, with only Martha's family and a few close neighbors in attendance.

He kept to himself during the time of mourning and silently accepted food from his friends. Lazarus went several times to talk with him. A few weeks later, Martha was standing by her gate when she turned to see Nathan walking toward her. He was pulling a small cart loaded with goods.

She eyed the cart. "Good morning, Nathan. Are you traveling?"

"I will say goodbye. I am sorry about the death of your father. He was a man of honor."

Martha looked at him in astonishment. "You are leaving Bethany?"

He cleared his throat. "I'm taking some things of my wife's to the home of relatives in Capernaum as was her final wish. I'm not sure when I will return."

Martha sensed he wanted to say more. There was an awkward silence, and then she said, "I wish you a good journey, Nathan, and thank you for the kindness to my father. He valued you as a friend."

The dark eyes studied her briefly but were unreadable. Finally he just nodded his head solemnly, then suddenly his face became stern and his eyes bore into hers. "May all you do in the days to come honor his name," he said sternly, and turning away, strode quickly down the road, leaving her staring after him. She knew what he meant, and she didn't know if she was angry or frightened.

She closed the gate more firmly than necessary and, grabbing the broom, began sweeping the courtyard with a vengeance.

The weeks dragged by and still there was no word from Thaddeus. She went to the olive grove on the Sabbath, but she waited alone. She wondered how far his band of soldiers would have to travel seeking this Barabbas.

It was in the middle of the fifth week, just after their evening meal, when there was a firm knocking on the gate. Lazarus rose, and with a glance of apprehension at his sisters, went slowly to open it. Martha moved protectively toward Mary and her heart pounded. Who would knock so loudly? Could it be soldiers? What had they done?

A Roman soldier did indeed stand at the gate, but he was alone. It was obvious he was uncomfortable and tried to cover the awkwardness with a gruff manner.

"I am Marcus, in the service of Captain Flavious. I seek a woman called Martha at this house. Is she here?"

Martha hurried to the gate, her fear giving way to gladness. Thaddeus must have sent her word of some kind.

"I am Martha. Do you have news for me?"

The soldier seemed startled at her quiet presence, giving her the idea that he'd expected another type of woman. Finally he nodded and pulled something from his pouch. "I have come on behalf of Captain Flavious. We were engaged in battle against a group of rebels and he was severely wounded."

Martha stared at him and fear began to well up in her heart. "Captain Flavious, he is recovering?"

Seeing her stricken face, the soldier's gruffness softened. "I promised him I would come here to tell you in person. The battle was hard, and just as we were gaining on Barabbas and his band, one of their arrows found its mark and the captain suffered a mortal wound. He seemed to be recovering, but then his condition became worse. There was an . . . infection. He died of his wounds, two days ago. I'm sorry." The soldier took a scroll out of his tunic along with something wrapped in a soft cloth.

"He told me the words to say that he could

not . . ." The young man struggled with his emotions for a brief moment. "He was the finest soldier I ever knew." He held out the scroll and cloth, and when she slowly took them, he turned abruptly and walked away, leaving Martha staring down at the scroll. She slowly unwrapped the cloth and found a gold medallion that shimmered in the palm of her hand.

Mary came and put her arm around Martha, who stood numbly, unable even to cry.

Lazarus gently took the scroll from her and unrolled it. She would want to hear the words and Martha could not read. The captain must have known Lazarus would be the one to read it, for to their surprise and relief, it was written in Hebrew.

My beloved,
I have little time. I thank our God for you and that I have known love once again in my life. Whatever you would have decided I knew I could live with, for I carry you in my heart. May you keep this medallion, a gift from my father to remember me by. I go to our God.
Farewell, my love,
Thaddeus

When he'd read the last word, Lazarus carefully rolled up the scroll and put it back in her hand. Mary led her across the courtyard and eased her down on a bench by the house. She sat, clutching the scroll and medallion, as Mary stroked her hair and Lazarus knelt in front of her.

"I am so sorry, Martha. Forgive me for the harsh words I spoke to you. You had decided, hadn't you?"

She nodded her head slowly. "I could not let him go."

Mary looked at Lazarus with a puzzled expression. "Is this the Roman soldier who saved our father's life?"

"Yes," he murmured quietly.

Suddenly Mary's face lit with understanding. "I wondered about those Sabbath afternoons."

Martha's voice came out in a cracked whisper. "I would like to be alone for a while."

Mary hugged her and went into the house. Lazarus stood and gave his sister a sorrowful smile. "You know, for what it is worth, I wanted you to be happy."

Then he too went to his bed.

Martha sat still for a long time, reliving the moments in the olive grove with Thaddeus, the sweet words, his strong arms around her, the thoughts of his villa in Cyprus. Yes, she had decided to marry him, for she didn't want to live without him. Now it didn't matter. He was gone and love went with him. She knew she couldn't grieve for Thaddeus openly, but with her father's recent death, no one would question her grief.

The tears flowed freely now and she didn't wipe them away.

She fell to her knees with her arms around herself, rocking back and forth. Anguished cries rose up in her throat and she longed to cry aloud. Finally she stuffed her gathered cloak against her mouth and moaned softly. "Thaddeus, Thaddeus, my dear love," she whispered as her body shook with grief. She stayed that way for a long time until she slid forward and lay uncaring on the cold, packed earth.

"Oh God Who Sees, take me also. If not together in life, let me join him in death. I don't want to live without him."

She awoke sometime later, chilled to the bone. She opened her hand and looked at the medallion for a long moment and then clutched it to her heart. His hands had held this. It had been about his neck.

She looked up at the night sky. Had the God Who Sees kept her from making a mistake? Would it have worked out the way she dreamed? Could she have left Mary and Lazarus and gone off to Cyprus with Thaddeus? Now she would never know.

She forced herself to get up and, wiping her face on her cloak, walked unsteadily toward the house. As she entered, she was relieved to find her brother and sister still asleep. She looked about for a place to keep her treasures and her eyes fell on the small chest. She opened it quietly, and down in a corner, under her mother's wedding dress, she placed the scroll and medallion and then closed the lid.

Martha felt sure no one else in their village knew of her meetings with Thaddeus but Lazarus and Nathan. They would keep her secret, Lazarus because he was her brother and loved her, and Nathan because her father had been his friend. He would not bring shame on Ephraim's family.

As she slowly sank down on her pallet, there was a movement from Mary, and Martha turned to find her sister awake.

"I'm sorry. I didn't mean to wake you."

"It's all right, Martha, I could not sleep. You wanted to be alone, so I did not disturb you." Mary rose and came to her sister. She knelt down and put her arms around her. "Oh, Martha, I'm so sorry."

The two sisters held each other for a long time as a bird's sweet song from the sycamore tree wafted through the shadows, heralding a new day that was to come.

12

Lazarus slammed the gate and stood in the courtyard, his hands balled into fists at his sides.

Martha saw the look on his face and hurried over. "My brother, whatever has happened? You look terrible."

"There will be no wedding."

She stepped back in shock. "No wedding? What has changed your mind?"

His shoulders sagged. "Tekoa, the nephew of Shaul and Helah, who is visiting from Bethlehem."

She shook her head, trying to understand. "What does Tekoa have to do with the wedding?"

"I saw Shua with him in the grove of sycamore trees. They were standing close together. It was the look on Shua's face—she has never gazed at me like that."

"You think she cares for him? But she is betrothed to you, Lazarus. If she has behaved improperly, that is a serious matter for the Elders."

He shook his head slowly. "No, there must be another way."

Just then there was a loud knocking at the gate and Martha opened it to find Shua and her father, Neziah. He still wore his leather potter's apron and there was dried clay on his hands.

"My daughter has been weeping ever since she came home and she will not tell me why." He pulled the frightened girl into the courtyard and glared at Lazarus. "What have you done?"

Lazarus looked at her sadly. "Will you tell him?"

"I meant no harm," Shua stammered.

Lazarus sighed. "She was in the grove with Tekoa."

Neziah turned to his daughter. "What were you doing in the grove with him?" He grabbed her by the shoulders, shaking her.

"I . . . I have been meeting Tekoa, the nephew of Shaul and Helah, in the grove. Lazarus saw us together."

Martha put her arm around Shua. "You must tell us, Shua. Have you and Tekoa done anything that would bring shame on your family?"

Shua sniffed and wiped her eyes on her shawl. "We have not done anything wrong. We've only talked. He has not even touched me." She began weeping again, pleading with Lazarus. "You must believe me."

Neziah's eyes flashed. "You have shamed yourself and our family. You should not even be alone with another man. You are betrothed." He raised his arm as if to strike her and Lazarus stepped forward.

"No. I do not believe she has done anything

wrong." He searched the stricken girl's face. "Is it Tekoa your heart has chosen instead of me, Shua?"

She looked up at him hesitantly and, seeing the compassion in his face, nodded her head.

Lazarus's shoulders slumped and he stood looking down at the ground a long moment. Then he turned to Neziah. "The matter is done. Let us resolve this in a quiet way. I will go into Jerusalem and procure a bill of divorcement for Shua. I will say I chose not to be married at this time. You can pretend anger and say you will seek a more suitable husband. Then you can travel to Bethlehem and make arrangements with Tekoa's parents." Lazarus thought a moment. "Tekoa should return home immediately so there is no chance of scandal. I will suggest that to him quietly to-morrow."

Neziah stood for a long moment, looking at Lazarus and then his daughter. Finally he shook his head slowly. "You would save our family from shame. I have no words. You are an honorable man, Lazarus. I will not forget." He gave Lazarus a sad smile. "You would have made a fine son-in-law. May the God Who Sees bless you for your kindness."

Shua was looking up at Lazarus, her eyes wide. "You would do that for me, Lazarus?"

He put a gentle hand on her shoulder. "Perhaps God has something else in mind for me, Shua. We will leave it in his hands."

Neziah turned to his daughter. "Let us return home. You will not leave our house until I travel to Bethlehem and the arrangements are made. If you see Tekoa again before this matter is attended to, I will not be responsible for the outcome. Do you understand?"

"Yes, Father." She sniffed.

Neziah bowed to Lazarus and they left.

When the gate closed, Martha turned to Mary, who had been standing near the house, listening with wide eyes. "You will not speak of this to anyone, Mary. It must remain quiet."

"I would not betray our brother, Martha. You know that."

His brave demeanor melted as Lazarus sat down suddenly on a bench and put his face in his hands. Mary went and put her arms around his shoulders.

Martha stood looking at both of them. Was there no end to the sorrow her family must bear? Would they be able to keep this quiet as they hoped? The next few days would tell.

Lazarus went to speak with Tekoa. When he returned, Mary had gone to her pallet for the night and Martha sat in the courtyard contemplating all the things that had happened in the last few weeks.

Lazarus motioned for Martha to come near. He glanced around them quickly and then whispered,

"There may be trouble. Faced with the circumstances, Shaul confessed the reason that Tekoa was there. He has traveled with the rebels."

"The rebels?"

"Barabbas."

She gasped. "The robber Thaddeus and his men were seeking?"

"That is the one."

Fear gripped her heart. "Is our village in danger, Lazarus?"

"Shaul does not believe the soldiers recognized Tekoa, for in the battle he became frightened and stayed back in the trees. He doesn't think he was seen. He returned home, but his parents sent him to his uncle as a precaution."

"Lazarus, they are crucifying any of the rebels they've caught. This could bring the Roman soldiers down on our village if they know he is here."

"We must not fear, sister. We must believe the soldiers do not know him, or where he is. It is good that his parents persuaded him to stay out of sight."

"Then he cannot return to Bethlehem."

Lazarus shook his head. "This will complicate my plan for Shua." He sat down suddenly on the bench. "What shall I do, sister?"

She put a hand on his shoulder, comforting her brother as he had comforted her only a short time before.

Lazarus suddenly pounded his fist into his palm. "I think I have a plan that would work."

Martha shook her head. "You'd better go and talk with Shua's parents. Who knows what they will agree to do."

"Under the circumstances, I think they will agree." He hurried from the courtyard.

When Lazarus returned an hour later, it was with relief.

"Shua's parents have agreed to my plan, as did Tekoa. We will all leave early in the morning for Jerusalem."

"We?"

"Tekoa, Shua, her parents, you, Mary, and my-self. We will be less conspicuous if there are women in the group. We will ask Hanniel if we can have the wedding performed in his court-yard. Will you go?"

It was fall, the month of Tishri, and they had just been to Jerusalem to celebrate the Festival of Tabernacles.

"Lazarus, I have work to do. We have been gone nearly a week. How will Hanniel welcome us so soon after hosting us for Sukkoth? How can we impose on Hanniel and Sherah again?" She stared at him while all the negative things she could say passed through her mind.

"Sister, we must go. We will find Rabbi Abraham to marry Shua and Tekoa, then they will slip out of the city. Shua's aunt and uncle in Hebron have been sent word. They will go there."

"Lazarus, the city will still be crowded with pilgrims from Sukkoth, and where there are crowds there are more soldiers. It would be dangerous for all of us. What if they recognize Tekoa?"

They argued in whispers, but in the end, she agreed. If Lazarus could do this for Shua in spite of his hurt, she could do this for Lazarus.

When Lazarus had gone to his bed, she went up on the roof and, falling on her knees, implored the God Who Sees to protect their village and her home. "May Lazarus's plan work for all of us." A soft breeze brushed her face and the turmoil in her heart subsided. Comforted, she knew now that she would never marry. She would remain in Bethany and take care of her family every way she knew.

Lazarus and Tekoa glanced around furtively as the small group gathered the next morning. Shua, her face drawn and fearful, was dressed in white homespun and a soft, blue mantle. She carried a small bundle of her belongings on her arm. Her parents, Neziah and Saffira, were tight-lipped and silent. As an additional precaution, Tekoa wore a dark cloak to hide his face. Mary was not feeling well, and Martha was reluctant to leave her alone at home. At Lazarus's whispered urging, Martha finally agreed to go to Jerusalem. She assured

Mary they would be home as quickly as possible.

Mary went to Shua and embraced her. "I wish you well as Tekoa's wife. I would have liked to have you for my sister-in-law, but I understand." She turned to Lazarus. "I will feed the animals if you are delayed."

Shaul bade his nephew goodbye and turned to Lazarus. "You have my deepest apologies for bringing this sorrow to your house. We had no idea when we agreed to shelter our nephew that it would cause so much grief."

"Thank you for your kind words, Shaul, but are not all things in the hand of God?"

Shaul nodded and turned away sadly.

The small band walked down the road, and Martha hoped fervently that they appeared to be just an ordinary family group going to Jerusalem. Tekoa walked between Lazarus and Neziah, his head down and the cloak pulled about his face. Shua walked with her mother and Martha.

Saffira shook her head sadly. "I know we must do this, for both your sakes, Shua, but you are my only child. When will I see you again? I pray our message reaches my sister and her family in Hebron. I only told them to expect you and your new husband. I told them nothing else. You will have to deal with that when you arrive."

"I am grateful for all you and Father have done. You will see me again. I will send you word when we have arrived safely. We will be all right, I promise." Then she added softly, "I love him, Mother."

Martha listened to their whispered conversation and felt her heart soften toward Shua. Had she herself not contemplated a life far from her own family with Thaddeus? How could she judge Shua?

As they neared the entrance to the city, Lazarus noted the crowds moving toward the Temple.

Lazarus frowned. "What is happening? The Festival is over." They stopped at a fruit seller's stall. "Why are the people gathering again at the Temple?"

The man shook his head and shrugged. "That rabbi is back, the one that caused such chaos in the Temple at Passover. He came the last day of Sukkoth and now teaches in the courtyard of the Gentiles. It is said he heals all who come to him." He looked furtively around. "I myself think he is a sorcerer."

Lazarus raised his eyebrows but thanked the man and turned to Martha. "Perhaps you women should go to the home of our cousin, Hanniel, with Tekoa. If there is trouble, we don't want him around any Roman soldiers. I will seek out a scribe and obtain the bill of divorcement for Shua. Then we will have to find a rabbi willing to perform the wedding ceremony."

They all agreed that, to explain the hasty wedding, they would say Tekoa must travel to

Hebron to begin his apprenticeship with a relative and wanted to take his bride with him.

Hanniel was surprised to see his relatives again.

Martha nodded to him. "Peace be upon this house."

When Martha told him their purpose, he glanced at his wife and shrugged. "It has been a long time since we have had a wedding. How can we refuse two young people our hospitality?" He agreed to allow the wedding in their courtyard.

Martha presented the date and raisin cakes she'd packed. Saffira brought fresh bread and two bottles of wine. Sherah went to her storage room to see what else she could prepare quickly. Hanniel hurried to find two other men to hold the canopy, if Lazarus and Neziah could find a rabbi who would come. Tekoa sank down on a bench in a corner of the courtyard, looking bewildered and saying little. Shua went to sit beside him, shyly looking at his face. He finally turned to her and they began to talk in hushed tones.

The group waited anxiously for Lazarus and Neziah to return. Martha feared another scene in the Temple with the unknown rabbi like the one that had occurred at Passover. As she looked around at the others, she saw concern on their faces as well.

Her relief was almost palpable when Lazarus and Neziah returned and Rabbi Abraham was with them. Lazarus slipped the bill of divorcement into Shua's hand. She looked at him a long moment, bereft of words, and her eyes pooled with tears as she tucked the document in her bundle of clothing. While the rabbi glanced at Shua with raised eyebrows, he did not question her. Lazarus murmured to Martha that Neziah had paid the rabbi well to perform the wedding.

The rabbi looked around nervously. "I must return to the Temple as soon as possible. That strange new rabbi is stirring up trouble among the people. I pray he does not feel the need to cause another riot in the Temple courtyard."

Martha saw her brother lift his eyebrows in interest and glance eagerly toward the Temple. What was he thinking?

Some of the neighbors arrived and two young men along with Lazarus and Hanniel held the canopy. Neziah led Shua around its perimeters and finally entrusted her to Tekoa.

It was the shortest wedding ceremony Martha could remember, and the most solemn. The rabbi had hardly finished the ceremony when he took his leave and hurried back to the Temple. The few guests wished the young couple well and, after partaking of the less-than-bountiful array of food and wine, left for their homes. Martha sensed that Neziah was embarrassed to marry off his only child in this way. Shua's mother had no doubt dreamt of the day her daughter would marry, with joyful music and dancing. The parents put on a brave front and smiled until the last guest was gone, then Saffira burst into tears. Neziah tried to comfort her, but Martha could see by his face he was in need of comfort himself.

Tekoa and Shua gathered their things, and Saffira wept openly as she embraced her daughter for the last time. Neziah embraced his daughter briefly and turned to Tekoa, his face stern, almost harsh. "I don't know you well, young man, but you are now my daughter's husband. I entrust you with her care."

Tekoa nodded to his new father-in-law and, drawing himself up, bravely faced the group. "I will take good care of Shua. I do love her. I apologize for all the trouble I have put you all through." He turned to Lazarus. "Not many men would do as you have done. I will remember your kindness to Shua and me the rest of my life." He turned back to Neziah. "When we get to Hebron, I will send word of our safe arrival."

It was a long speech for Tekoa, and Neziah put a hand on his shoulder. "That is good. We will look for word from you." He reached into his belt and pulled out a small leather pouch. "You will need this for food and lodging. Keep it out of sight and be sure to find safe lodging before darkness falls."

Tekoa stared at the pouch and then took it from Neziah's hand. "I will be careful with it."

The young couple thanked Hanniel and Sherah

for their kindness and hospitality and, with a final wave to all, went through the gate and, in moments, were lost in the crowd.

Martha watched them go, praying silently that God would watch over them and give them a safe journey.

Hanniel turned to Lazarus. "Will you stay the night? You are more than welcome."

Lazarus glanced quickly at Martha. "We thank you for your kind offer and all you have done, but Mary is home alone and we must return as soon as possible."

Hanniel sighed and glanced at his wife. "Much is going on in Jerusalem these days. Be careful, my young friend; may God go with you."

As soon as they were out of sight of the house of Hanniel, Lazarus turned toward the Temple.

Martha's eyes widened in alarm. She reached out and put a hand on her brother's arm. "My brother, we need to go home. Mary is there alone."

Lazarus brushed off her hand. "Mary will be fine, and besides, you know you are curious as well." He grinned at her outrageously.

"Lazarus, what are you doing?"

"I wish to hear this new rabbi. I have heard stories in the marketplace of things he has done." He turned to Martha and there was excitement in his voice. "I heard from someone who has seen those things that the fruit seller was right—this man performs miracles of healing wherever he goes."

Martha shook her head and her apprehension grew. She covered her head with her shawl and struggled to keep up with Lazarus, who was pushing his way through the crowd like a donkey headed for his stall.

13

Martha stayed close to her brother as he worked his way through the crowd. Finally he was only about thirty feet from Jesus. Lazarus pulled Martha to the shadow of a pillar where they could slip away easily if there was trouble and yet they could clearly hear what the rabbi was saying.

She studied the rabbi. What was there about him that caused such interest? He was somewhat tall and his hair was parted in the middle after the custom of the Nazarenes, his complexion made darker by long hours in the sun. His beard was thick and fell to his shoulders in tight waves. His appearance was not unpleasant. His eyes were like dark mysterious pools, now flashing, now filled with compassion. He did not appear to be a charlatan but a man intent on motivating his audience. She leaned against the pillar and listened.

Jesus was speaking to the Pharisees. "You search the Scriptures, for in them you think you have eternal life, and these are they which testify of me. But you are not willing to come to me that you may have life. I do not receive honor from men, but I know you, that you do not have the love of God in you. I have come in my Father's name and you do not receive me; if another comes in his own name, him you will receive. How can you believe, who receive honor from one another, and do not seek the honor that comes from the only God? Do not think that I shall accuse you to the Father; there is one who accuses you—Moses, in whom you trust. For if you believed Moses, you would believe me, for he wrote about me. But if you do not believe his writings, how will you believe my words?"

The leaders murmured among themselves and cast him hard looks but did not reply. They turned on their heels and stalked away from him. He shook his head sadly and turned to the people.

Lazarus questioned the man next to him. "The leaders seem upset. Has he done anything wrong?"

"You just arrived. Jesus healed a paralyzed man by the pool of Bethesda, near the Sheep Gate."

"He has healed before, so I've heard. Why would this infuriate them?"

The man sighed. "Jesus did it on the Sabbath. It is unlawful to heal on the Sabbath."

Lazarus looked at Martha and back to the man. "Jesus did another miracle, caused a paralyzed man to walk, and they are angry because he did it on the Sabbath?"

"That is what happened."

"Thank you for your information, friend."

There was a stir among the crowd as people began to bring the sick and crippled to Jesus. Lazarus and Martha watched incredulously along with the crowd, who gasped and applauded each miracle as if they were watching a performance. Martha stood transfixed by what she saw. Jesus had only to touch them and they walked away healed. Who was this man, she asked herself? What power did he have and where did it come from if not from God?

Martha.

The voice was gentle and she looked around to see who was speaking to her.

It came again. *Martha.*

Just then the rabbi looked directly at her, and while he didn't speak out loud, she heard the words.

I'm coming to your house today.

She was dumb with astonishment.

The crowd began to disperse when they realized the rabbi was going to leave the Temple courtyard. Before Martha could stop him, Lazarus strode forward and stood in front of the rabbi. She couldn't hear what Lazarus said to him, but suddenly Jesus smiled and put a hand on Lazarus's shoulder, nodding his head.

When Lazarus returned to where Martha was standing, he grinned. "Let us return quickly to

Bethany. I have invited Jesus and his disciples to come to our home."

Martha looked at him incredulously. "I'm to prepare a meal for all of them?"

"Cooking is what you do best, Martha. Come."

Her sputtering was to no avail. In moments they were out of the Temple, and once again Martha could hardly keep up with Lazarus as he eagerly set out for home. She shook her head. He had invited this strange rabbi and his disciples, and she would have to honor his invitation and feed their guests. With a sigh she set her mind to figuring out what she had on hand and what she could prepare quickly. Then she thought of Mary. Was she better or worse since they left this morning? If she was still not feeling well, she wouldn't be much help. Martha would have to do it all herself. Suddenly she couldn't wait to get home and tell Mary who was coming.

They were both out of breath when they reached their gate, and Lazarus went directly to the storeroom to see how much wine they had on hand. Martha saw Mary sitting on her favorite bench, waiting for them.

"Mary, I need you. We are having guests for dinner. Are you well enough to help me?"

"I am much better, sister. Who is coming to our home?"

"The rabbi who has been doing miracles around the countryside. Your brother invited him . . . and his disciples. There will be thirteen of them and they are on their way."

"Jesus is coming to our home?" Mary's face lit up with joy. "I have heard of him. The whole village is talking about the miracles he does."

"Well, it will take a miracle to get ready for all of them. Go and find all the cushions you can and lay them around the table. I'll start a lentil stew. Bring the basket of dates and the goat cheese in the stone jar. Then gather some leeks from the garden."

As Mary hurried away to do her bidding, Martha gathered garlic, dill, mustard seeds, vinegar, and olive oil. She sliced the cucumbers she'd picked the day before into cubes and put them in a bowl with olives, red wine vinegar, and chopped dill. She sprinkled the cucumber with crumbled goat cheese and set the bowl hastily on the table. Then she put out two loaves of bread and sent Mary to get another loaf from a neighbor.

As the lentils cooked, she added coriander seeds, bay leaves, salt, and vinegar, along with olive oil and garlic.

Mary no sooner completed one task when Martha gave her another. "See how many date cakes we have in the other stone jar." She looked heavenward and prayed there would be enough to go around. There were fifteen cakes. She breathed a sigh of relief.

True to her word, Mary had fed the animals,

saving Lazarus time. He quickly set wooden cups and pitchers of wine on the table.

There was a gentle knock at the gate. They were here!

Lazarus opened the gate.

The rabbi smiled warmly. "Peace be upon this house."

Lazarus welcomed Jesus and his disciples to their home. Martha glanced at the men who traveled with Jesus. They looked weary and she regretted her unkind thoughts earlier. Could she not show hospitality to a man of God and his followers? When had they last had a good meal? With renewed vigor, she went about her tasks.

As the men settled in the courtyard, speaking quietly among themselves, Jesus smiled at Martha. "It is good of you to let us partake of your bounty. Let me introduce my disciples."

As Martha stood quietly, Lazarus came to stand by her side. Mary hurried over to join them.

"This is Matthew, our record keeper. He used his pen for Herod once, gathering your hard-earned money, but now he writes down what he sees for our records. We couldn't do without him."

Matthew was a burly man, not tall, but with a piercing gaze that told Martha he missed little around him. A tax collector? Martha held the smile on her face. Obviously the man had made a great change in his life to follow Jesus. Matthew nodded to them.

"This is James and his brother John, my sons of thunder. Once they fished the sea, but now they are fishers of men."

The two men smiled in acknowledgment. Martha could see the family resemblance in their dark auburn hair, their almost square chins and bushy eyebrows that shadowed piercing brown eyes. They were like two controlled bodies of energy, and she had no doubt that Jesus had to keep an eye on them.

"This is Thomas."

The young man grinned at the three of them and bowed his head briefly in acknowledgment. Martha noted that his eyes rested the longest on Mary. To Martha's dismay, Mary was returning his gaze with delight. He was almost as tall as Lazarus, with curly black hair that threatened to cover his eyes. His smile was warm and open and Martha found herself liking him.

"This is Peter and his brother, Andrew. They were also fishermen and still help to feed us when we are near the sea."

Andrew gave them a friendly smile. Martha sensed that he was a trustworthy man who said what he thought. Peter, on the other hand, was a big man with great arms from hauling in fishing nets. His dark hair, barely held back by his headband, threatened to spill into his face. Martha sensed power there, subdued perhaps around Jesus, but she wondered if he had a temper. He wouldn't be a man to be crossed.

Jesus waved a hand at each of the next four men. "These are Philip, Nathaniel, James, the son of Alphaeus, and Simon, formerly a zealot, who now serves the kingdom."

Suddenly two men entered hastily through the open gate, interrupting Jesus. "Peace be on this household."

Jesus sighed. "And this is Judas, son of James, and our treasurer, Judas Iscariot."

Martha noted the young Judas and found herself wondering what his mother thought of him traipsing all over the country with an itinerant rabbi. He beamed at her and she returned the smile. Then she observed the other Judas. The one Jesus had called Iscariot. His face was bland and frown lines were visible around his mouth. He had a bag of coins tied to his girdle and looked warily at Lazarus. He acknowledged the three but did not look Martha in the eye. He glanced around the courtyard as if assessing the value of their possessions and home. She decided he was a man to watch. It also occurred to her to wonder why he was following Jesus. He seemed uncomfortable and found a quiet place to sit alone and observe them all.

When the introductions had been made, Lazarus invited their guests to gather around the table. Jesus asked a blessing on the food and the household that had welcomed them. Mary brought out bowls of water for the ritual hand-washing, and finally they began to eat. The women hurried around the table, setting out food. The men broke the bread and passed it around. As they tasted the dishes Martha had prepared and dipped their bread in the lentil stew, there were smiles of appreciation.

As Mary helped serve, Martha saw Thomas observing her sister with open admiration. When he glanced up and saw Martha watching him, he busied himself with his food.

Then, as Mary placed a basket of raisin cakes on the table in front of him, he gave her such a beaming smile that it almost brought tears to Martha's eyes. She thought of when she and Thaddeus had first met and the warmth that filled her unexpectedly in an instant. If it was so with Thomas and Mary, nothing could come of it. He was traveling the road with Jesus and probably had little to his name. Nevertheless, with thoughts of Thaddeus in mind, she spoke gently to her sister.

"Mary, would you bring the basket of almonds from the storeroom?"

Mary looked up and their eyes met. Martha was sure Mary had no idea what she was thinking, but Mary gave her a smile of such understanding before she turned away. Martha stood still a long moment before her thoughts came back to the present, and she placed the dish of olives she was holding on the table.

When all had eaten their fill and had as much wine as Lazarus could offer, the men leaned back with the ease of well-filled stomachs and talked among themselves.

Lazarus reclined at the end of the table near Jesus. Martha was so busy serving that she wasn't able to hear what they were talking about. Lazarus was looking at Jesus with adoration. For a moment Martha felt a jolt of fear. What if Lazarus decided to become a disciple and leave their home to travel about the country with Jesus? She came closer and, with the pretense of seeing if they needed anything more, tuned her ears to their conversation.

With sudden clarity she realized Jesus knew what she was thinking. He looked up at her and she was aware of a sense of kindness and great love.

She glanced over at Mary, who was talking to Thomas in a corner of the courtyard. The two young people looked up at her briefly as if sensing her gaze. Then Lazarus spoke to Jesus, and the words caused Martha to turn back with alarm.

"Master, let me follow you. I want to go with you."

Martha's heart jolted within her. She wanted to cry out, *No, we need you here. I cannot do it all myself.* Sudden tears stung her eyes. She kept her head down lest anyone see she was upset but watched from the corner of her eyes, straining her ears to hear the Master's answer.

Jesus put a hand on Lazarus's shoulder. "I know, my young friend, but you are needed here." He became solemn for a long moment. "There will come a day when you will serve me, Lazarus, but it is not your time yet."

Martha's relief was palpable. She hurried into the storeroom to have a moment to gather herself together.

The disciples, enjoying a respite from long hours on the road, were in a mood to celebrate. Thomas pulled a *kinnor,* a small harp, from his sash and began to plunk its strings, sending a simple melody through the courtyard. Mary picked up her lyre and joined in the music. Jesus seemed to be thoroughly enjoying himself, his eyes dancing with the music. Martha suddenly felt like celebrating with them.

As the hour grew late, Jesus rose from the table and his disciples, ever aware of his movements, rose with him.

Martha hated to see him leave. "Master, you are welcome to sleep here."

"You are kind, Martha, and a generous hostess, but we will retire to the Mount of Olives for the night."

"Will you come again?"

He smiled and she was lost in the depths of his eyes. "I must travel a long way, but whenever we are in this area again, we will come."

Lazarus came to the gate. "You are welcome anytime, Master. Our home is yours."

Jesus glanced over to where Thomas and Mary were talking quietly. "I believe at least one of my disciples has good reason to return also." His eyes danced and Martha was filled with love for him—not the love she'd known with Thaddeus, but a holy love, deep and abiding. It didn't matter what others said about him. She knew who he was.

14

After Jesus and his disciples left them to return to the region of Galilee, Martha and her family returned to their regular tasks. Everyone praised God to think that Jesus had come to their village. Many who had loved ones who were sick or infirm asked anxiously if Martha knew when Jesus would return. She could only shake her head.

Lazarus worked the fields and continued to make bricks for the village, but Martha was aware that he traveled into Jerusalem as often as he could to glean news of Jesus's travels. There were those coming south who were only too anxious to share what they'd seen and heard.

Martha marveled as Lazarus shared the stories of the blind receiving sight, the lame healed, demons cast out. Her eyes widened in astonishment as Lazarus told her of two people who had even been raised from the dead.

As the family sat quietly in the courtyard one evening, Lazarus sighed heavily. "There is other talk, sisters. He is angering the religious leaders everywhere he goes. He shows them up for the callous and unfeeling windbags they are. Whitewashed bones, he calls them. Now there is a rumor that the Sanhedrin is looking for a way to get rid of Jesus."

Mary gasped. "Would they do him harm? Have him arrested?"

Martha was irate. "He's done nothing wrong, except heal the sick and preach about the kingdom of God."

Lazarus nodded. "I know, but since the priests cannot live up to the prophecies, they feel they have to get rid of this prophet. There is trouble brewing, I can feel it whenever I walk about the city. Those who follow Jesus's teachings are watched with suspicion."

"Are we in danger, Lazarus?"

"I don't think so, at least as far as I know. We can only watch and see."

In an attempt to lighten the heavy mood, he turned to Mary with a slight grin. "Have you heard from Thomas?"

Mary blushed. "He sends me word when he can. He and the other disciples were with Jesus near Capernaum but starting for Galilee again. I don't know where they are right now."

Lazarus rose. "That is good. They are heading south. That means they will return here, I'm sure of it." He yawned and stretched. "Time for a good night's sleep." He turned to Martha. "Are your weavings prepared for tomorrow? I'll take them into Jerusalem with me."

She nodded. "They are ready. Perhaps tomorrow you will have more news of where Jesus and his disciples are."

Martha looked toward Jerusalem and remembered the first time she heard Jesus's voice. He told her he was coming to her house that day, and he did. Now, with a certainty in her spirit, she knew he was coming again, and she and Mary set to work getting ready for his arrival. With an almost unspoken agreement, Lazarus moved out of his father's room and it was prepared for Jesus. A comfortable pallet, a small table, and her father's oil lamp. One of Martha's best woven rugs was placed on the dirt floor and Mary brought in a jug of field flowers to be placed in the corner of the room.

Martha was anxious for news of the Master, and when Lazarus returned from the city, she hurried toward him. He stood with his head down in the open gateway.

Martha stopped suddenly. "What is wrong? What have you heard?"

He looked up at her and shook his head sadly. "Herod has beheaded John the Baptist."

Martha felt like someone had struck her in the chest. "Why did he do that? He left him alone for so long."

Lazarus pursed his lips and closed the gate firmly, too firmly. "The daughter of Herodias, as wicked as her mother, danced for the king, and the drunken old man was so taken with her that he promised her anything she wanted. A servant girl from the palace said he promised her half the kingdom. She went to her mother, who told her to ask for John's head on a platter. It appears the king couldn't back down on his word in front of his court." He sat down on a bench, staring at the ground.

"I have a bad feeling about this, Lazarus. Wasn't John the Baptist a cousin to Jesus?"

"He was."

"Do you think the leaders are going to figure out a way to kill Jesus?"

"That is the talk among the believers in Jerusalem."

Mary approached, having heard the last of the conversation. Her face was white with alarm. "Who is going to kill Jesus?"

Martha put a hand on her arm. "Your brother was just saying that the leaders don't like how he is portraying them, and word is they are plotting ways to get rid of him."

"Then he must stay away from Jerusalem, for his own safety."

Lazarus sighed. "That would be our solution, Mary, but Jesus will do what he feels led to do, even if it puts him in danger."

Martha turned her practical mind to a more basic issue. "What happened to the body of John?"

Lazarus got up and started toward the animals. It was time to feed them. "His disciples came and got the body. They buried him," he called over his shoulder.

He will come, Martha told herself. He would need a quiet place away from the crowds, to rest and strengthen himself.

Mary touched her arm. "Should we not prepare for the Master?"

The two sisters prepared food and stored it away. Mary kept the room swept and clean, and the family waited.

Then he was there, standing in their courtyard and greeting them warmly. Only three of his disciples were with him: Thomas, who was unmarried; Judas, son of James; and John. She looked past him, seeking the rest of his band.

"They are with their families for a time."

Martha realized that she was glad that Judas Iscariot was not with them. His brooding presence last time had made her uncomfortable.

Thomas gazed at Mary, who shyly lowered her eyes, but not before Martha had seen the gladness leap to her face.

Lazarus embraced Jesus. "Master, I grieve for you over your cousin, John. We have heard of his fate and have prayed earnestly for you."

Jesus put a hand on Lazarus's arm. "Thank you, my young friend. Your prayers are needed." He gave Martha a grateful smile, seeing her concern. He also turned to Mary, whose eyes were full of love for him as she came and knelt at his feet with a bowl of water.

"Master, let me wash the dust from your feet after a long journey."

It was the job of a servant, but Martha had no servants. She was tempted to say something, but recognized the rightness of Mary's actions.

Mary washed Jesus's feet and then the feet of his three disciples, lingering on Jesus and then Thomas, who submitted reluctantly. She dried each set of feet with a cloth.

Jesus looked down lovingly at her. "Thank you, Mary, for your kindness."

Mary gave a deep sigh at his words of praise and rose to empty the bowl of dirty water. She brought fresh water from their storage jar for all to wash their hands.

The men reclined on cushions at the table in the house for the coolness of the month of

Hesvan, the fall of the year, was upon them. Rains had been intermittent, and Lazarus had been busy plowing the fields and getting ready to plant the grain. Soon the olive harvest would be upon them when all three of the family would glean what they could from their small grove of olive trees.

Martha had brought her clay cooking stove into the house and cooked in the room that would have been Lazarus and Shua's. Lazarus had made an opening in the roof for smoke to escape, but the house was full of cooking smells.

While Jesus exhibited his usual cheerfulness, weariness showed in his eyes. Though he laughed with them and listened to the stories Thomas and John told about the miracles Jesus had done, he seemed somehow detached from them, his mind elsewhere.

Thomas was telling them about the trip into Samaria. "We tried talking him out of it, but he was adamant. We didn't want to go there, since we have nothing to do with the Samaritans, but the Master prevailed. He sat at Jacob's well and waited while we went into town to buy food." He looked around as the disciples nodded. "Let me tell you, I didn't want to go into Shechem, but what were we to do?"

Judas took up the story. "When we returned, there was the Master, talking with a Samaritan woman. We remained quiet, but certainly wondered why he was talking with a woman, and one alone at this well. It wasn't even the town well."

Thomas shook his head. "We had a feeling she was a woman with a questionable reputation." He glanced at Jesus, who was listening with a slight smile playing about his lips.

Young Judas laughed. "Next thing we knew, she dropped her water jug and ran back into the town. We weren't sure what was going to happen next, but in a short time she returned and brought half the town with her."

Mary broke in. "Did they mean you harm?"

Thomas shrugged. "No, they wanted to hear what Jesus had to say. They even invited us to come into their town and tell them about the king-dom of God." He shook his head, thinking about it. "We stayed two days, and many came into the kingdom because of the Master's teaching."

Martha looked at Jesus with wonder. What an amazing man he was. Never had she met a man with such compassion and love for those in need.

Story after story took up most of the evening. When the first stars came out in the gathering dusk, Martha went to Jesus. "We have prepared a room for you, Master. We—Mary and I—felt it was right. Will you stay?"

The warmth in Jesus's eyes was all the answer she needed as he looked up at her and nodded. He wished them a good evening and went into the room she indicated, closing the leather flap behind him. The other three disciples made their pallets as best they could in the main room, separating themselves on the other side of the room from Martha and Mary. Lazarus slept between the two groups for propriety's sake.

The small group stayed for two days, and Martha sensed a change in Jesus, a determination, yet peace of spirit. She knew when he left the house in the wee hours of the morning to seek a quiet place alone to pray and when he returned. Then it was time for them to go.

"I must return to Capernaum. The rest of my disciples will join me there." He embraced Lazarus and turned to smile gently at Martha and Mary. His eyes were like deep pools and Martha felt herself lost in their depths.

"I will come to Jerusalem again at Passover."

Martha turned to him, anxiety filling her heart. "Master, is it safe for you in Jerusalem? There are rumors that the leaders plot to get rid of you."

"Martha, do not be concerned for me. My time has not yet come and I have more work to do for the Father. No harm will come to me until I have finished what he sent me to do."

Chastised, she lowered her eyes. He tipped up her chin with one finger. "Watch the road, Martha. I will send someone to you shortly who will bring you great joy."

She gave him a puzzled glance but could not bring herself to ask him to elaborate. She would trust and wait.

Mary and Thomas spoke quietly in the corner of the courtyard and their faces spoke of the sorrow of parting again. Mary would have to be content until Jesus returned with his disciples, and no one knew when that would be.

As the family watched Jesus and the three disciples walk up the road and turn toward Bethphage, Martha knew at least this time that he would not be going through Jerusalem.

Lazarus went toward the village to see a neighbor about repairing a wall, and Mary returned to the house to finish carding the wool from their sheep. Later she would spin it into thread, then tomorrow she and Martha would dye the thread for the loom.

Martha remained at the gate, looking down the road and wondering what Jesus had meant. Who was she watching for?

15

In the month of Adar, the main rains were over. It was early spring. The fields of flax were ready for the harvest and the almond trees were in blossom. The sun shone warmly on the village as Martha returned from the shop of the potter. She needed a new cooking pot, for the old one had cracked beyond repair. She stopped at the garden and gathered some herbs. As she reached her gate, she set the pot down to open the gate and, hearing voices, looked up to see two men coming down the road. They were some distance away. She smiled to herself. It was hard to miss the size and build of Nathan the blacksmith. He was returning to Bethany after a long absence. Men had needed his skills and were forced to go to the next village to have tools repaired. He would be welcomed back. She was glad to see their family friend again. She couldn't make out the identity of the other man and stood shading her eyes from the sun to see him better. There was also something familiar about him, the way he walked . . . she couldn't put her finger on why, but she felt she knew him.

As the men approached, Nathan stopped and greeted her with a puzzled look on his face. "Good morning." He seemed surprised to see her. Then she remembered the day he left and his warning. He'd known about her liaison with Thaddeus. Nathan had been gone. He didn't know. She smiled at him and answered, "Good morning, Nathan. The men of the village will be glad you have returned."

Then she turned to his companion, and as he flung back the hood of his cloak, the basket of herbs slipped from her fingers and scattered on the ground.

Simon!

For once Martha had no words. He was not

wearing the veil over his face nor was there any sign of his illness. He looked hale and hardy— his old self—yet instinctively she took a step backward.

"No need to fear me, Martha. I no longer have leprosy. I found Jesus in Galilee." He shook his head. "He seemed almost to be expecting me. He touched me and the leprosy was gone."

Martha's eyes widened at his words as she realized it was true. There was no sign of the leprosy. His skin was normal and his face and arms brown from the sun but without spots or lesions.

"Oh Simon, how wonderful for you!" she cried. Her heart nearly burst with joy, realizing what this would mean to his family and to her dear friend, Esther. She turned back to Nathan as he spoke, and his voice was softer.

"I am glad you are still here. You made the right choice then, didn't you?" he said.

She lifted her chin. "There was no choice to make, Nathan. My friend died in battle." She could say it matter-of-factly now, without the deep pain. Thaddeus was with God.

His eyes widened with surprise but only for a moment, then he nodded sagely. There was no judgment on his countenance.

She turned to Simon. "How did you and Nathan meet?"

"He was heading for Jerusalem and home. I recognized him and called out. When he heard

140

my story, he welcomed me as a brother and bought me some food. He also bought me some clothes so I would be presentable to my family. Nathan has walked the rest of the journey with me."

Martha had not missed the word "brother." She turned to their old friend. "Are you a believer, Nathan?"

His eyes shone, the fierceness of his former countenance gone. "I saw Jesus in Bethsaida and watched miracle after miracle. I believe he is the Messiah. The one we have looked for so long. Yes, I am a believer."

She put a hand on his arm. "We are also believers, Nathan. Jesus and his disciples have stayed at our home. We too believe he is the Messiah."

Nathan nodded his head vigorously. "That is good news. Many changes have occurred since I left."

Simon moved restlessly, impatient to be off, and she knew he was anxious to see his wife and family again.

Martha nodded. "There is joy in our village today. God has done a wondrous thing. Hurry to your family, Simon."

As the two men continued down the street, there were voices calling out as neighbors recognized Simon. People came out of their homes and crowded around him. Martha hurried into the courtyard and found Mary. When she told her who she'd been speaking with, Mary could hardly contain her joy. She was almost dancing as she followed Martha out to the road where people swarmed behind Simon as he neared his house. They didn't want to miss this.

Judith stepped out into the street to see what was happening. When she saw Simon, she clasped a hand to her mouth, staring at him as though he were a ghost.

"I am healed, wife. There is no more leprosy."

When she finally found her voice, Judith could only cry out, "Simon!" before falling into his arms. The women of the village, including Martha and Mary, wept openly, and even burly Nathan had tears in his eyes. Chloe came out to the gate, and when she realized who it was, hung back, not sure what to do.

Mary hurried to her side. "Your father-in-law has returned to his family. He is healed."

Judith, through her tears, murmured, "Tobias is in the fields."

"I will go and find him," someone called out. The crowd parted as the runner sprinted toward the fields of flax that were ripening in warm sun.

The men came in from the fields all around, and in a few moments, Tobias was striding down the street. When he saw his father, he broke into a run and was clasped to his father's chest.

"Father, oh Father. You are home at last," Tobias cried with tears streaming down his face.

Neighbors crowded around, clapping Simon on the back and praising God for his goodness and mercy.

"Tell us what happened," Shaul asked.

The villagers quieted down and looked at Simon expectantly. They didn't want to miss a word.

Simon stood with his arms around his wife and his son. "I was near the Sea of Galilee and heard about this rabbi, Jesus, who was performing miracles and healing people of all kinds of diseases and infirmities. When I learned he was coming near where I was, I went and without thinking of my status as a leper, flung myself down at his feet. He asked me what I wanted him to do. I said, 'I want to be healed so I can return to my family.' He asked me if I believed he could heal me."

Martha remembered the same words Jesus had spoken to others before he healed them. Believing played a great part in healing, she determined.

Simon continued. "He reached out and touched me. He had no qualms about touching a leper. He just smiled and touched me. Instantly I felt heat go through my body and I looked at my hands that were whole again. The flesh was as if I'd never had leprosy. I knew I was healed totally and fell down at his feet. He lifted me up and said, 'Return to Bethany, to your family, Simon.' He knew who I was. Is this not the Son of God? The Messiah?" Simon looked around at his neighbors, who were nodding their heads and murmuring assent. How could they not believe when this marvelous miracle had been done? Were they not witnesses to the day Simon had left them and sadly walked away? Now here he was, restored to health and returned to his family.

"Have you been declared healed, Simon?" This from one of the village elders.

"Yes, I have been to the priest in Jerusalem, and he has declared me whole again and given permission to return to my home and family." He waved his arm at his friends. "Let us celebrate and rejoice at God's goodness."

The women hurried home to gather food and the festivities began. They sang, ate, and danced until nearly dark. Even Nathan joined the men as arm in arm they moved in a line to the music. Martha was amazed at the change in Nathan. He laughed and danced, and Martha was surprised. Nathan was almost handsome.

As the people dispersed to their homes at last, Tobias and Simon saw them out the gate and thanked them for sharing in their joy.

Lazarus had joined them when he heard the news and embraced his friend Tobias. "God has seen his affliction, and rendered his mercy."

Martha, Mary, and Lazarus finally started home. Lazarus carried an oil lamp he'd borrowed from Tobias. When at last they reached their home, Martha picked up the basket and the wilted herbs from the stone step in front of the gate and

Lazarus brought in her new cooking pot. It had been a day to remember.

Mary unrolled her pallet, her face still shining with the excitement. She turned to Martha for a moment. "I'm not sure I can handle any more miracles. It takes one's energy." She gave her sister a wry smile and wished her good night.

It was only when she settled herself to sleep that night that Martha remembered the words of Jesus. "Keep watching the road, I am sending someone who will bring you great joy."

It had indeed been a day of great joy. Suddenly she sat up. Esther! She and Micah were in Bethlehem. She had not seen them since the Passover nearly two months before when they had come with their small baby son they had named Zeri.

Martha smiled at the memory. How Judith had rejoiced in the pleasure of having a grandson.

Tobias had chortled. "I'm an uncle, and soon I'll be a father myself." His wife Chloe was expecting a child in a few months. Everyone took turns holding the baby. As Mary held the baby, she told Esther and Micah about Jesus's visits to their home and shared stories of the miracles he had wrought.

Micah stroked his beard. "I would hear this man. Surely a man who can do such things is sent from God."

"He was here, Micah, at the home of Martha,

Mary, and Lazarus. We heard him ourselves. When he comes again, we will try to send you word."

Martha, watching her sister cuddle the baby and coo to him, suddenly realized again that Mary was eligible for marriage. Then another thought occurred to her. Mary could have children. There were eligible young men in their village. Yet another thought inserted itself. Mary was in love with Thomas. Her face lit up like a menorah whenever she saw him. It was hopeless, but what could she say? Mary would have to come to that conclusion herself.

Esther placed the baby in Martha's arms, and as she looked down, the child seemed to study her intently. Then he smiled and her heart overflowed. How good it felt to hold a child in her arms. For a moment she saw the earnest face of Thaddeus in her mind, telling her about the villa in Cyprus and what a good place it was to raise a family. She clasped the small bundle to her heart and willed the thoughts away. He was gone and with him the dream of children of her own. She looked up and saw Esther watching her with a sad, sweet smile of understanding. Martha smiled back. She kissed little Zeri and handed him reluctantly to Judith, who waited anxiously to hold her grandson again.

Micah beamed with pride, overjoyed to have a son at last. He and Tobias laughed and celebrated as Tobias clapped him on the back, congratulating him. Martha rolled her eyes. You'd think Micah had produced this baby all by himself.

When Micah and Esther had to return home, Martha felt the loneliness sweep over her heart again. Then she looked over at Chloe. She'd almost forgotten. Soon there would be another child to hold and cuddle.

Now as she lay on her pallet and thought of her friend, Martha realized someone must send Esther and Micah word at once. Esther's father was healed and had returned home. The whole village had celebrated Simon's healing, but Esther didn't know. She looked over at Lazarus. "Brother, someone must go to Bethlehem and bring Esther."

He yawned and with a voice heavy with sleep, murmured, "Someone has already gone. They will reach Bethlehem tomorrow."

She lay back down but looked at the ceiling for a long time. So much had happened. What would tomorrow hold, and when would they see Jesus again?

16

In the month of Tishri, at the beginning of the first fall rains, Martha learned Jesus had come quietly to Jerusalem for the Feast of Tabernacles. Yom Kippur had ended and at the beginning of the Feast, five days later, her family had obeyed the Word of the Lord and lived in a shelter made of palm branches and woven coverings for seven days. She loved the joyous celebration in Jerusalem and knew it spread to all the towns and villages as God's people observed this sacred holiday. Lazarus returned from Jerusalem and told Martha that over seventy oxen had been sacrificed in the Temple.

Now, as Martha folded the coverings and Lazarus took the booth apart for another year, Mary came back from the village well. "Word is spreading through the village. Now that the Feast of Tabernacles has ended, Jesus will be teaching again at the Temple."

Martha sighed. "That will mean more crowds to hear his teaching." She'd observed that while many came for enlightenment or healing, most came out of curiosity.

Mary agreed. "They hope to see one of his miracles."

Martha and Lazarus made plans to travel into Jerusalem to hear the Master. This time Mary would accompany them.

It was a two-mile walk to the city with Lazarus striding out eagerly, causing Martha and Mary to hurry to keep up with him. By the time they reached the steps to the Temple and found a place to stand to hear Jesus, Martha was out of breath. She glared at her brother, to no avail.

Jesus was in the middle of teaching on forgiveness when there was an interruption and the people parted, murmuring to themselves as a group of scribes and Pharisees strode up to Jesus, dragging a young woman with torn clothing. The girl was weeping and trying to cover herself with her arms when they threw her down in front of Jesus. She slowly, painfully struggled to rise and ended up on her knees before Jesus.

One of the Pharisees stepped forward, a sneer on his face. Martha was startled by their angry mood. The faces of the men with him were hard, and there was something else, a sense of anticipation. They were almost licking their lips, their eyes intensely focused on Jesus.

"Teacher, this woman was caught in the very act of adultery."

Martha was irate and looked around. "Where is the man who committed this act with her?"

Lazarus gave her a sharp look that suggested silence.

The Pharisee went on. "Moses, in the law, commanded us that such should be stoned. What do you say?"

The crowd seemed to Martha to wait with almost palpable silence for his answer. Yet he said not a word; he merely stooped down and wrote on the ground as if he hadn't heard them.

When they continued pressing their question, he raised himself up and looked at the group of men, his expression one of pity.

"He who is without sin among you, let him be the first to throw a stone at her." He then stooped down and again wrote on the ground.

The group of scribes and Pharisees reacted as though they had been struck. They turned to each other with startled looks on their faces.

"What kind of an answer was that?" one of the scribes whispered.

Someone in the crowd began to chuckle and a titter spread through the courtyard. The scribes on the outside of the group turned and walked hastily away. One by one the other men in their group followed them until the one Pharisee who had led the delegation flung up one hand in exasperation and stalked out of the courtyard.

Then all eyes turned to Jesus and the young woman who knelt with her head down in front of him.

Jesus raised himself and looked after the retreating scribes and Pharisees. "Woman, where are those accusers of yours? Has no one condemned you?"

The woman answered fearfully, "No one, Lord."

Jesus reached out and lifted her chin so that she could look into his eyes.

"Neither do I condemn you; go and sin no more." He scanned the crowd as if looking for something, and finally a young woman stepped forward, offering her cloak to the trembling woman who stood before Jesus. He thanked her and covered the girl's bare shoulders.

"Thank you," the girl whispered. She slowly stood up and straightened herself and with her eyes never leaving Jesus's face, nodded slowly. Then she turned and with her head up, and a light in her eyes, walked through the crowd that parted almost respectfully as she passed by.

Jesus resumed his teaching but was interrupted again by another Pharisee. "You bear witness of yourself, your witness is not true."

He looked at the man for a moment. "Even if I bear witness of myself, my witness is true, for I know where I came from and where I am going; but you do not know where I come from or where I am going. You judge according to the flesh; I judge no one. And yet, if I do judge, my judgment is true; for I am not alone, but I am with the Father who sent me. It is also written in your law that the testimony of two men is true. I am One who bears witness of myself, and the Father who sent me bears witness of me."

Another Pharisee scoffed. "Where is your Father?"

"You know neither me nor my Father. If you had known me, you would have known the Father also."

Mary turned to Lazarus. "They heckle him. Will they try to arrest him?"

He shook his head. "They are just testing him. I

151

don't think they will do anything with all the people present."

After another session of words with the Pharisees, Jesus shook his head. "I am going away, and you will seek me, and will die in your sin. Where I go you cannot come."

The leaders standing near Martha murmured to themselves. "Will he kill himself, because he says, 'Where I go you cannot come'?"

Jesus answered their thoughts. "You are from beneath, I am from above. You are of this world; I am not of this world. Therefore I said to you that you will die in your sins; for if you do not believe that I am he, you will die in your sins."

"Who are you?" someone in the crowd called out.

"Just what I have been saying to you from the beginning. I have many things to say and to judge concerning you, but he who sent me is true, and I speak to the world those things which I heard from him."

People were shaking their heads. Martha listened along with her brother and sister and tried to understand what he was saying.

Jesus spoke again. "When you lift up the Son of Man, then you will know that I am he and that I do nothing of myself; but as my Father taught me, I speak these things. And he who sent me is with me. The Father has not left me alone, for I always do those things that please him."

Thinking of all the miracles he'd done, and listening to him, not only in their home but here, Martha affirmed to herself, *He is the Messiah. The One we have waited for all these many years.*

As another of the religious leaders began to question Jesus, he leaned over to Thomas and whispered something. Thomas smiled, nodded, and slipped through the crowd to where Martha, Mary, and Lazarus stood.

Thomas reached Mary's side. "The Master requests me to tell you he wishes to come to your house tonight."

The two young people stood for a moment looking at each other before Mary found her voice. "Thank you, Thomas, we will be glad to have him . . . and all of you too."

Thomas reluctantly left Mary's side to return to be near Jesus. The disciples were grouped around, not enough to keep him from the people, but to observe the crowd with watchful eyes, ever protective of their Master.

Martha and her family needed to return home, for there was work to be done. She was already planning the meal in her head. At Lazarus's signal, the three slipped through the crowd and were soon out of the city on the road to Bethany.

The two sisters worked feverishly to make sure the house was ready. Lazarus returned to the fields to check the barley planting, but when he came to the house at the end of the day, he was nearly ready to return to the fields.

"Martha, Jesus is coming to see us as a friend. He is not going to inspect our house for dust."

She made a face at him and went on vigorously sweeping the courtyard and sent Mary to take inventory of their storeroom, to see what they had on hand.

Lazarus tried to stay out of the way of his sister's zealous efforts, and it was almost with relief when he responded to a familiar voice at the gate and welcomed the Master into the courtyard.

Not wanting to attract a crowd, Jesus wore a dark cloak and brought only three of his disciples, Thomas, Matthew, and Judas Iscariot. Martha learned the others were again with their families in Jerusalem. The small band greeted the family warmly—with the exception of Judas Iscariot. His smile did not reach his eyes as he dipped his head in acknowledgment and then slipped past them to sit in a quiet corner again. Martha looked after him a moment, but with so much to do she returned to her tasks. Over Mary's whispered protests, Martha sent her again to check the storeroom.

Simon, his wife Judith, Tobias, and Chloe, as well as their friend Nathan, were quietly summoned, and they slipped into the courtyard after darkness had fallen. Martha's small courtyard could not contain all the villagers who would crowd in to see and hear Jesus if they knew he was there.

Martha brought fresh-baked bread out of the oven with the wooden paddles and slid it onto the table to cool. A bowl of fresh fava beans, simmered to tenderness, was poured into a bowl with onions, olive oil, garlic, vinegar, and cumin. She added a dash of salt and placed it on the table along with a bowl of brine-cured olives. Millet had been cooked with dried almonds, raisins, and small green onions. She had added chicken to their usual lentil stew and the aroma of the various dishes filled the courtyard. Just then, she looked for Mary to have her put the wooden platters on the table, but her sister was nowhere in sight.

Martha frowned. Where could she have gone? With the group of men gathered around Jesus, Martha had to look twice before spotting Mary sitting at the Master's feet, listening intently to his words. Indignation rose up in her breast. *Am I to feed these men all by myself?* She strode over to the group gathered in the shady side of the courtyard and, without thinking, interrupted Jesus as he was talking on prayer.

"Lord, do you not care that my sister has left me to serve alone? Please, tell her to help me."

Jesus paused and looked up, his dark eyes taking in her expression as she stood with her hands on her hips. A smile tugged at the corners of his mouth as he looked from Martha to her sister.

"Martha, Martha, you are worried and troubled about many things, but one thing is needed, and Mary has chosen that good part, which will not be taken away."

She took a step backward, feeling the rebuke, and struggled to retain her composure. Tears of frustration threatened to escape her eyes, and she held them back by sheer willpower. Slowly she sank down on a nearby bench, unsure of what to do.

Mary looked at her sister with a gentle smile. "Jesus was telling us about prayer and the prayer he's taught his disciples."

Martha took a deep breath and, seeing no condemnation in the eyes of Jesus, ventured, "I . . . I would like to hear that prayer."

Jesus seemed pleased with her request. "The prayer I've taught them is this: Our Father in heaven, hallowed be your name. Your kingdom come, your will be done on earth as it is in heaven. Give us this day our daily bread and forgive us our sins, for we also forgive everyone who is indebted to us. And do not lead us into temptation but deliver us from the evil one."

Martha contemplated the words. "That is a good prayer, Lord. I will remember it." She rose almost timidly and spread one hand toward the table. "I pray you, come and partake of the meal, refresh yourselves."

Mary rose quickly then and brought the bowls

of water so they could all wash their hands.

Once again, talk flowed around the table of the places they had been and the miracles Jesus had done.

Matthew spoke up. "We thought there would be retaliation by the Sanhedrin when the Master healed a blind man the first day of the Feast of Tabernacles. It was the Sabbath and the man had been born blind."

Martha paused in her serving as Lazarus asked, "You say the man had been born blind? Did he have eyes?"

Matthew waved a hand. "Yes, he had eyes, but they were almost pale, milky colored. It was obvious he couldn't see."

Thomas spoke thoughtfully. "We were sure that the man or his parents had committed some terrible sin for him to be born blind. What did we know?"

Simon, sitting at Jesus's right hand, turned to him. "But what did you say?"

"That neither he nor his parents sinned, but that the works of God should be revealed in him."

Matthew laughed. "You should have seen the faces of the crowd when the Master spat on the ground and mixed it with clay, then he put the clay on the man's eyes and told him to go and wash in the pool of Siloam."

Mary burst out, "And then what happened?"

Thomas looked down at the table, remembering.

"He washed off the clay and came back seeing."

Martha and Mary gasped at once.

Lazarus, on Jesus's other side, leaned forward. "You said you thought the Sanhedrin would do something? What happened then?"

Judas, who'd been quietly listening, spat out, "The religious leaders couldn't believe their own eyes. They thought it was a trick of some kind and after questioning him over and over, finally had to call his parents to ask them if the man was truly born blind. When they affirmed that he was, they still wouldn't give credit to the Master. They wanted him to just give God the glory, calling Jesus a sinner." He pounded his fist into his hand, causing all to jump. "Instead of acknowledging that a major miracle had been done, they were angry."

Lazarus shook his head. "Why were they angry?"

Judas leaned back, a sneer on his handsome face. "Because it was done on Sabbath. When the man insisted Jesus must be from God to do such a miracle, they actually threw him out of the Temple."

Martha pondered this story in her heart. As she heard of the confrontations with Jesus and the religious leaders, a sense of apprehension grew. Sooner or later the leaders would act, but when? She and Mary gathered the empty platters to clean them and, after removing the main dishes and bread from the table, replaced them with date cakes and a platter of fruit. Lazarus poured wine into their wooden goblets, but none of the disciples drank to excess. Jesus only sipped his wine with his meal and they followed his example.

Simon insisted that the next time Jesus was in Bethany that it was his turn, out of gratitude, to host Jesus at his home, and Jesus agreed that he would be there.

Martha and Mary quietly cleaned up after the meal, and Martha then settled down on a nearby bench to listen to Jesus as he shared with his disciples and taught all of them the truths of being a good shepherd. He compared himself to the shepherd and the people to the sheep the shepherd watched over.

"I am the door," he told them. "If anyone enters by me, he will be saved, and will go in and out and find pasture."

Martha realized the pasture was heaven. Jesus was the way to heaven. She sighed contentedly, surveying her courtyard and the men who were sharing it with her family. She thought back to the time she had decided to run away with Thaddeus. It was not to be. If she had gone, she never would have had the opportunity to meet and hear Jesus. The God Who Sees knew her life and ordered her days. Whatever was to come, she knew she could trust him.

She looked over at Mary and Thomas, sitting

together in a quiet corner of the courtyard, near but not touching, absorbed in Jesus's words. Whatever tomorrow might bring, it was in God's hands. A small breeze wafted through the courtyard as she sat very still, holding this moment and this night to her heart.

17

After his brief visit with Martha and her family, Jesus left quietly with his three disciples in the early hours of the morning and went to the Garden of Gethsemane to pray. They would visit other towns and villages before returning to Jerusalem.

Now the twenty-fifth of the month of Kislev had arrived, the time for the Feast of Dedication. Martha, shivering with the winter cold, moved the small cooking stove indoors.

She called out to the courtyard, "Mary, will you get the menorah from the storeroom? I imagine it needs polishing."

"I have it already," Mary called back.

Martha went to the door. Mary was already vigorously polishing the candleholder to a high shine. Shaking her head, Martha went back to setting up the winter cooking area. Sometimes she had to remember that Mary was not a child who had to be told what to do. Mary had taken over half the load of work off Martha's shoulders.

That afternoon, Martha finished the sash she'd woven for Lazarus. Mary's was already finished and wrapped in a cloth. They were the only gifts she'd be giving her brother and sister during the eight days of Hanukkah. Fortunately they were able to go about their usual work, for no tasks were forbidden or unlawful during the festival of lights, except on the Sabbath.

That evening when Lazarus returned, they lit the *shamash,* the guard candle, and then used it to light the first menorah candle.

Martha gave Mary and Lazarus their sashes that evening. Mary gave Lazarus and her sister each necklaces she'd made from beads—a large dark brown bead to represent the earth, with smaller black beads on either side on a leather cord for Lazarus. Martha's necklace was made of small lapis lazuli–colored beads. Lazarus, as keeper of the money of the household, gave Martha and Mary a small leather bag of coins. Though some families gave gifts to each other each night of the Feast, Martha suggested they not try to do that.

"After all, there are no children in the household," she reasoned.

The family did give small gifts to Tobias and Chloe's little girl, Reza, a top and a small doll made of fabric scraps, which Mary had carefully sewn.

There was no window facing the street, so the

family placed the menorah each evening on a stand in the courtyard where it was protected from the cold night breezes, and those passing by could see its light.

The house was filled with the cooking smells of special foods that were prepared during the season.

Mary sang as she fried the potato pancakes in olive oil. Martha had made the jam-filled doughnuts that Lazarus loved. She had to admit she loved them herself and ate three that morning.

They all loved the special cheeses, and Martha unpacked them from the crocks where they had ripened.

It was a festive time in Bethany with neighbors wishing each other *"Gemar chatimah tovah."* "May you be sealed totally for good."

Lazarus wanted to hear Jesus again, and on the fourth day of the Feast, the family went into Jerusalem where Jesus walked and talked in the Temple on Solomon's Porch. As he again taught the people, the Jewish leaders taunted him.

"How long will you keep us in doubt? If you are the Christ, tell us plainly."

Jesus answered, "I told you and you do not believe. The works that I do in my Father's name, they bear witness of me, but you do not believe because you are not of my sheep, as I said to you. My sheep hear my voice, and I know them, and they follow me. And I shall give them eternal life, and they shall never perish; neither shall anyone snatch them out of my hand. My Father, who has given them to me, is greater than all; and no one is able to snatch them out of my Father's hand. I and my Father are one."

To Martha's horror, some of the Jews in the courtyard took up stones, and she realized they were going to stone him. She and Mary shrank back against Lazarus, her heart thumping so loud she thought someone could hear it.

Jesus faced his foes calmly. "Many good works I have shown you from my Father. For which of those works do you stone me?"

Someone shouted from the crowd—it was one of the scribes.

"For a good work we do not stone you but for blasphemy, and because you, being a man, make yourself God."

Jesus stared him down. "Is it not written in your law, 'I said you are gods'? If he called them gods, to whom the word of God came, do you say of him, whom the Father sanctified and sent into the world, 'You are blaspheming' because I said I am the Son of God? If I do not do the works of my Father, do not believe me, but if I do, though you do not believe me, believe the works, that you may know and believe that the Father is in me and I in him."

Some of the Jews made as if to seize him, but he walked calmly through the midst of them as if they were standing still and, with his disciples following, left the Temple.

Martha stood amazed and looked at her sister and brother.

Lazarus was shaking his head. "If I had not just seen this with my own eyes, I would not have believed it. They were ready to stone him, yet as he passed by, no one made a move."

"It is because of who he is," Mary murmured.

Martha looked toward the Temple gate where Jesus left. He was now out of sight. "Yes, sister, I believe you are right."

The crowd broke up and the three made their way back to Bethany. Many of their neighbors walked with them and the men murmured quietly among themselves. Martha and Mary walked in silence, absorbed in their own thoughts.

When the Feast of Dedication ended, word came to the village that Jesus and his disciples had returned to the land beyond the Jordan where John had baptized, and he would remain there for a while, teaching and healing those brought to him.

Martha worked hard on her loom to finish a second rug for Lazarus to take into town. They could use the money, for feeding so many had caused their food supply to dwindle quickly. With the rains, Lazarus had not been able to do much brick-making or work on anyone's home. He spent time with Nathan at the blacksmith's shop and helped him with some work, just to have something to do. He developed a slight cough. As it worsened, he waved away Martha's concerns.

"Lazarus, you must wear a warmer cloak when you go out."

"I'm warm enough, sister. Do not worry about me."

Martha kept her peace but caught Mary's concerned look as the cough deepened and settled in his chest.

That night, Martha awoke as Lazarus tossed fitfully on his pallet. She rose and hurried over, putting a hand on his brow. He was hot with fever. She put cool cloths on his forehead and tried to get him to sip some water. When daylight came, Mary, who had watched through the night with Martha, ran to fetch Anna, the healer.

Anna made a compound of some of her herbs and mixed them with hot water. Lazarus took only a little and the rest dribbled down his chin. Anna tried poultices on his chest, but the fever did not abate. Nathan came to inquire and was alarmed as he looked down on Lazarus's flushed face and glazed eyes.

"I did not realize he was this ill. Has Anna, the healer, not been able to help?"

Martha shook her head. "She has done all she can. The fever rages no matter what we do."

The two sisters and Nathan prayed fervently for his recovery, and finally Martha rose from her knees. "We must send for Jesus. The Master will know what to do. Has he not laid hands on the sick and healed them? Lazarus is his friend, he will come."

Nathan gathered himself. "I will go. He is in the countryside of Perea. I should not have trouble finding him." He looked down at Martha's stricken face and said gently, "I will bring him to you." He threw his cloak back on and rushed across the courtyard. As the gate swung closed behind him, Mary looked after him. "He is a true friend, sister. He will find Jesus for us."

Martha looked back at her brother and listened to his ragged breathing as he tossed about on his pallet. She murmured half to herself, "But will the Master get here in time?"

18

Martha awoke with a start and rubbed the back of her neck.

"Mary?"

Her sister looked up and gave a slight shake of her head. "No change."

"I didn't realize I'd fallen asleep. I'm sorry."

"You've hardly left his side in two days. You must rest sometime."

"And you?"

Mary gave her a wan smile. "I've dozed a little."

Mary went for some warm broth, and when she returned, Martha took the bowl and tried to spoon some into her brother's mouth.

"You must keep up your strength, Lazarus." She thought desperately for something that would reach him. "The Master is coming. He can help you."

To her relief, Lazarus opened glazed eyes. "Jesus . . . coming?"

"Yes, yes. He is on his way. Nathan went to find him."

Mary took one of Lazarus's hands, but he suddenly jerked it from her grasp, crying out incoherently. Martha bent down to try to understand him, but he seemed to be battling something she couldn't see.

Suddenly he became calm and Martha realized he had passed out again. The sisters sat watching his chest move agonizingly up and down as he struggled to breathe.

Martha watched her sister put another cold cloth on his forehead and found herself thinking back to when he was small. She was only four years older, yet she had always looked after him for her mother. Oh, the tricks he would play on her! She thought of the mouse he put in her pallet one night that caused her to wake up the neighbors with her screaming. He had been curious about everything, pausing to stoop to watch insects and small creatures in their courtyard. Once he caught a lizard by the tail, and she smiled to herself remembering his bewildered expression when the lizard fled, leaving his broken tail in the little boy's hand.

Mary suddenly spoke. "Are you all right, sister?"

Martha, startled from her musing, looked up. "I was just thinking of some of the tricks he used to play on us. He was always getting into mischief."

Mary nodded. "I was remembering the time he decided to ride our donkey, the one that had such a bad temper, and he promptly landed on his bottom. He sat gingerly for a while."

"And then there was the field mouse he put in my pallet one night."

"Oh Martha, I thought your screams would wake the entire neighborhood. You checked your bed every night for a month after that."

The two sisters smiled at each other briefly at the memory.

Martha looked down at Lazarus, still so young. She had ordered her brother and sister around since they were small and even after their father died. Yet in the last two years, Lazarus had become the male head of the household, and she began to defer to his judgment more and more.

Lazarus woke and Mary gave him sips of water. He slept again, his breathing so shallow Martha had to look twice to see if he was even breathing at all.

Martha rubbed her temples, the weariness and sorrow a weight upon her heart. How long could he endure this fever? Leaving Mary to watch over him, she went out to the courtyard and walked slowly to the gate. Where was Jesus? There was no sign of him, or Nathan. Did Nathan have trouble finding the Master? Had Jesus and his disciples moved to another area? Where were they?

As another day passed with no sign of Jesus, Martha's heart became like a stone in her chest. Didn't the Master care about them? He had called Lazarus his friend. They had spent many hours talking with one another. Surely at the first news of Lazarus's illness, Jesus would have left wherever he was ministering and hurried to them.

Fear subtly became anger, but Martha tried to wave it away. Jesus would come. He had to. He wouldn't let his friend die, would he? She pursed her lips. The frown on her face deepened as she gave free rein to the ugly thoughts.

Martha took turns with Mary, one staying with Lazarus, while the other prepared a meal or fed the animals. Both women slept little and weariness increased the silent tirade that tumbled through Martha's mind. She thought of all the times she'd prepared food over the last year for Jesus and his disciples, the hours cooking and baking. Now when they needed him, he did not come. And where was Nathan? Had he been waylaid on the road? Had he reached Jesus? The thoughts went round and round in her head until it ached.

A sense of apprehension clutched at Martha's heart. Her brother's breathing sounded like dry sticks rubbing together. "Keep fighting, Lazarus, don't give up!" she murmured. The heat and perspiration from his body told her the fever still raged. Her heart pounded as she called Mary to his side. Martha took one of his hands. Mary, her face mirroring her sister's fear, took the other.

Lazarus opened his eyes slowly and gave them a weak smile. He struggled to speak, and finally gasped, "Martha, Mary, dear sisters, I'm . . . sorry . . ."

"Sorry for what?" Martha cried. "Lazarus, speak to us."

He closed his eyes again, sighed, and lay still. His hands went limp in theirs.

"Lazarus?" Mary touched his face and looked up at Martha, tears rolling down her cheeks.

Martha slowly laid her brother's hand by his side and, choking back a sob, nodded her head. "He is gone."

The sisters reached for each other over the body of their loved one and wept.

Mary released her sister at last. "I must get Anna." She rose, steadying herself, and with a sigh, left the house.

Martha knew Mary's face and sad demeanor would tell the neighbors their brother had died.

Martha looked down at Lazarus a long moment.

He seemed as though he were sleeping. She turned and walked slowly out into the courtyard and sank down on a bench to await Mary's return. Her hair, normally bound up neatly, straggled down the sides of her face. Her shoulders sagged and her hands, which were rarely still, were clasped in her lap. What good would it do if the Master came now? The words echoed in her mind. *It is too late . . . too late.* Lazarus, his beloved friend, was dead. There was nothing to be done now but prepare the body for burial.

Anna came with haste, bringing ointment and spices, and the three women did what they needed to do with linen cloths and spices to prepare his body for burial. Martha sighed. She had buried her mother and father. Now Lazarus would join them.

The women worked with deft hands, for in the heat of the day Martha knew his body would decompose quickly. Mary's face was pinched and Martha moved in a daze, methodically doing what they had to do. When they were ready, Shaul, Tobias, and other men from the village came to carry the bier to the gravesite. The two grieving sisters walked with their arms about each other. Martha let the tears flow as she listened to their neighbors and friends cry aloud and cast dust in the air to show their sympathy and grief. The men placed Lazarus's body in the tomb and pushed the sealing stone in place.

Martha stayed with her sister, weeping and

receiving the comfort of their friends near the tomb. When at last the afternoon shadows began to drape over the rocks, the sisters made their way home. Women of the neighborhood brought food. Martha could not cook during the week of mourn-ing, neither did she care. The one she trusted, whom she had put her hope in, had not come.

Women took turns sitting with Mary, but Martha separated herself. The grief and pain were like a red-hot iron in her chest. She sat in a corner of the courtyard, eating only when her friend Esther's mother, Judith, brought her some stew and threatened to spoon it into her mouth. Martha's bitterness rose like bile in her throat as the days went by slowly and there was still no sign of Jesus or Nathan.

Mary tried to comfort Martha, but she too could only say, "If only the Master had been here."

Martha looked toward the gate. "I just don't understand. Why didn't he come?"

The days of mourning passed slowly. Then, on the fourth day after the burial of her brother, Mary sat in the house, surrounded by some of the women of the neighborhood, as she quietly played her harp. Martha remained outside in the court-yard, staring unseeing at the shadows on the wall.

Suddenly Judith rushed into the courtyard. She was nearly out of breath as she shook Martha's shoulder. "Jesus is coming! He is just outside Bethany."

Martha looked up slowly. "Jesus is here?" She sat still a long moment. What could she say to him? Could she vent the feelings that had gathered momentum during these last days? For the first time, the thought of having the Teacher and his disciples stay at her home brought a frown.

She stood up and nodded to Judith, who stood by anxiously watching her. Straightening her shoulders, she left the courtyard. She could not bring herself to hurry. There was no need to hurry now. Reluctance slowed her feet as she approached the small group of men, including Nathan, who stood quietly watching her.

All the angry things she had planned to say dissipated as she approached him and looked into his face. His eyes seemed to bore into her very soul. He knew her bitterness, yet there was no condemnation in his gaze. As the depth of his love poured through her, she could only fall on her knees and grasp his hand. The words tumbled forth from her heart. "Lord, if you had been here, my brother would not have died." She heard the reproach in her voice, yet as she looked up at him, a glimmer of hope stirred. "But even now I know that whatever you ask of God, God will give you."

Jesus lifted her to her feet. "Your brother will rise again."

Martha gave him a quizzical look. "I know that he will rise again in the resurrection, at the last day."

He smiled at her. "I am the resurrection and the life. He who believes in me, though he may die, he shall live. And whosoever lives and believes in me shall never die. Do you believe this?"

Did she believe this? Her mind raced as she thought of the recent dark days and the hope that had blossomed, faded, and then died as she waited for Jesus to come.

Jesus stood quietly, waiting for her answer. Did she still believe? She had seen the miracles. She had watched as Jesus healed the lame and sick. How could she deny his power? Lost in the depths of his eyes, to her surprise, like a ray of sunlight on a foggy morning, a sense of peace flowed over her. She felt her heart stir and, in spite of all she had gone through, saw her answer.

She spoke haltingly. "Yes, Lord, I believe that you are the Messiah, the Son of God, who is to come into the world."

"Would you fetch Mary?"

"Yes, Lord." She turned and walked quickly back to the house. Nathan caught up to her. She paused to let him open the gate, and then faced him. She had to ask. "Did you have trouble finding him, Nathan?"

He shook his head. "No, I found him quickly. When I told him, he merely nodded and said, 'This sickness is not unto death, but for the glory of God, that the Son of God may be glorified through it.' " Nathan frowned. "We stayed there two more days. I felt from his words that Lazarus would live."

"When you found him, did he realize how ill Lazarus was?"

"He knew. I made it clear. After the two days, he suddenly announced we were heading back to Judea. Then he told us Lazarus slept and he was going to wake him up."

"Wake him up?" Martha's eyes widened.

"Yes. Then Peter said, 'Lord, if he sleeps, he will get well.' "

"The Lord said Lazarus was asleep?"

"We misunderstood. Finally he told us plainly that your brother was dead, and that he was glad for their sakes that he was not there, that they might believe."

"And that's when you started for Bethany?"

"Yes, the disciples were concerned about the Jewish leaders and the danger to the Master." Nathan shook his head. "Thomas agreed they should all go, and if they died, they died."

Martha shook her head as fresh tears seeped out and streamed down her cheeks. "Thank you, Nathan." Her thoughts tumbled in confusion, but she said no more.

She entered the house and leaned over, whispering in Mary's ear. "The Teacher has come and is calling for you."

As soon as Mary heard those words, she gave a glad cry, laid aside her harp, and hurried to the gate. Unlike Martha, she ran up the road to where Jesus had waited.

Neighbors and friends who had been talking quietly, comforting Mary, watched her go and got up to follow her. As they passed Martha, she overheard one woman say, "She must be going to the tomb to weep. Let us go and weep with her."

Martha hurried to catch up with her sister.

When Mary saw Jesus, she gave a glad cry and fell at his feet as Martha had done. "Lord, if you had been here, my brother would not have died."

Martha saw Jesus look up at the crowd that surged toward him. A groan escaped his lips and his countenance was troubled.

He reached for her hands and lifted Mary as he had done with Martha. Sighing deeply, he asked, "Where have you laid him?"

Martha stepped forward. "Lord, come and see." At least the Lord wanted to visit her brother's grave.

Jesus followed the sisters, and as Martha glanced at his face, she was startled to see tears coursing down his cheeks.

The Jews around them murmured to one another, "See how he loved him!"

One of their neighbors who walked behind Martha murmured aloud, "Could not this Man, who opened the eyes of the blind, also have kept this man from dying?" Couldn't he?

The group approached the tomb, a cave with a

stone rolled up against the entrance. Jesus turned and gestured toward the grave.

In a firm voice he commanded, "Take away the stone."

Martha gasped. "Lord, by this time there is a stench. He has been dead four days."

He turned, and she felt the full impact of his gaze. "Did I not say to you that if you would believe you would see the glory of God?"

Bewildered, she turned to Nathan, who hesitated, but only for a moment. He motioned to Simon and Tobias, and the three men pushed until the large stone slowly moved away from the entrance to the tomb.

The people watching stepped back, covering their noses. Martha raised her shawl to her nose. The smell could be terrible. What was the Lord doing? Why would he put them through this agony?

Everyone watched Jesus expectantly. Tension buzzed through the crowd like a hive of bees.

Martha saw Jesus lift his eyes toward the heavens and heard him say in a voice that carried through the crowd, "Father, I thank you that you have heard me. And I know that you always hear me, but because of the people who are standing by I said this, that they may believe that you sent me."

Then he cried out, "Lazarus, come forth!"

Martha froze. She held her breath, her eyes

were riveted on the opening of the cave. Something was happening. She clutched Mary's arm, her eyes wide with fear. A shuffling sound was heard within the cave, and Martha saw what appeared to be a dark shape in the shadows. Then, to her astonishment, a wrapped figure moved slowly from the darkness of the cave and shuffled into the sunlight. Bound head and foot with the grave clothes, his face covered with the burial cloth, the figure stood swaying before them. The crowd gasped. There were shrieks of disbelief and some cried out in fear that it was a ghost. Others fell on their faces, giving glory to God.

Martha's fist went to her mouth. Her heart pounded and her mouth opened and closed but no sound came forth. Her feet felt as if they were rooted to the ground, but Mary, weeping with joy, hugged her.

Jesus waved a hand. "Loose him and let him go."

Mary pulled her forward. "Sister, our brother is restored to us."

Martha allowed Mary to bring her closer to the body. An odor seeped from the grave clothes as she reached out hesitantly to touch him. "Lazarus?"

A muffled voice answered.

Mary quickly pulled the cloth off his face, and Martha gasped as she once again looked upon her beloved younger brother. She and Mary began to frantically tear the wrappings from him. Nathan stepped forward suddenly to steady Lazarus as he was being set free. Nathan's eyes, wide with astonishment, looked at Lazarus, and he slowly shook his head. When at last Lazarus was free and he stood before them clad only in a loincloth, his skin nearly glowed with vitality. He smiled at his sisters and gathered them in an embrace. In her joy at the reunion, Martha realized there was no smell of death on him. His skin was healthy and pink.

Martha thought her heart would burst from her chest. "Lazarus, oh my dear brother, you are alive."

Lazarus examined his hands with wonder. "It would appear that I am." He turned as Jesus approached him and the two embraced.

"Master? Master," he repeated softly.

There were cries of "I believe!" "This is truly the Son of God!" People surged forward, wanting to touch Lazarus yet holding back. Was it a dead body that would make them unclean, or was he alive?

A few on the outskirts of the crowd took off on a dead run for Jerusalem. Martha, wiping her eyes on her shawl, saw them leave. Nathan also watched them leave.

"They will tell the leaders," he said firmly, "and now they will believe."

Martha's heart was filled with righteous

indignation. How can they not recognize Jesus as the Messiah? Who else but God could raise a man from the dead? She hung her head. "I doubted him, Nathan. I thought because he didn't come that he didn't care."

Nathan looked down at her. "Don't feel badly, Martha. How could you know what he intended to do?"

Tobias came forward and grasped Lazarus's hand. "Welcome back, my friend."

Martha turned to Chloe. "Go to our home and bring sandals, a tunic, and cloak for Lazarus."

His bare feet would be cut on the rocky road and the sun was rising high in the sky. The temperature soared. When the items were brought, Mary stooped to put the sandals on her brother's feet as he lifted the tunic over his head. Martha placed the cloak about his shoulders. Jesus walked with Lazarus as they slowly made their way back home. The crowd followed as they walked through the village. Some people reached out to touch Lazarus as he passed by. Some women wept, calling out blessings to him. Some smiled and murmured among themselves, and many loudly praised God for the miracle.

They entered the courtyard and as many as could crowded inside. Others stood outside the gate.

Martha saw the weariness on Jesus's face and turned to Peter who was standing nearby, her eyes pleading with him to do something. Peter's size could be as intimidating as Nathan's.

Peter drew himself up and turned to the crowd. "The family is grateful for your support and we rejoice with you at this blessing, but the Master is weary from a long trip, and our friend Lazarus must rest from his ordeal. Return to your homes and share this day's miracle with others."

Peter and the other disciples stood near the gate as some of the people reluctantly filed out, calling last-minute words of encouragement to Lazarus and glancing back at the still figure of Jesus, who did not refute Peter's words.

Some of their close friends and neighbors, including Nathan, stayed. Martha, still numb with shock, suddenly realized she must put together a meal. She glanced up as the men gathered together and caught Nathan's eyes as he seated Lazarus by Jesus. For the first time she became aware of the gentleness that replaced Nathan's usual stern countenance. With a sense of wonder, she thought of the many changes in their household and among their friends since Jesus had come.

She gathered bread, cheeses, ripe olives, fruit, and raisin cakes made during the last grape harvest. Mary put bread on the table as Martha stared down at the pot of lentil stew. It would give them something warm to eat, but was there enough to feed all of her guests? With a sigh she determined to serve what she had until it was gone.

She watched the pot as the men dipped their pieces of bread in again and again. When the pot should have been empty, there was still stew left. Shaking her head, she looked at the Master, who merely glanced up with a smile playing around his lips.

Jesus and his disciples remained at Lazarus's home for two days. From morning to evening, as many villagers as possible crowded into the small courtyard to see the Master and to observe Lazarus. Many still wanted to touch Lazarus and prove to themselves he was alive and well.

As the evening shadows fell the second evening, Jesus turned to Martha. "I must go. There are those who plot against me and I can no longer walk openly among the Jews. We will travel into the country, near Ephraim, and remain there for a while. I will come to you again soon."

"When, Lord?"

He looked toward Jerusalem. "Six days before the Passover."

Jesus embraced Lazarus warmly and smiled at the sisters. "Remember this day in the troubled days to come. It gave me joy to restore one I love dearly to his family."

"We cannot begin to express our gratitude to God for this great gift," Martha began but choked up with tears again.

Mary could only kiss the Master's hand and show her gratitude with her eyes.

When all had gone and the courtyard was quiet, Lazarus put an arm around his sisters. "I can hardly believe I am here with you again."

Mary looked up at his face. "What was it like, brother? Did you feel anything?"

He looked up at the star-glittered sky. "I was in a dark place, a place of silence, yet I felt no fear. Then I heard a voice calling my name and I awoke. I was able to sit up and I felt hands lifting me, moving me toward the entrance of the cave. Then I was standing in the sunshine, and you were unwrapping the cloths that bound me. When Mary took off the veil, I saw all of you, but then I saw the Lord." Lazarus's eyes were alight with wonder. "His clothes were shining like the sun itself and he was smiling at me. I knew I was alive and he'd brought me back from the grave."

Martha shook her head slowly as a sense of shame rose within her heart. "I doubted him. I thought that because he did not come right away, that he was not coming. And I couldn't understand."

Mary beamed. "Yet he knew all along what he was going to do."

Lazarus put a hand on Martha's shoulder. "I would have felt the same if it were you, dear sister. Do not sorrow for what is past. Let us rejoice in today and be thankful."

With a yawn, he turned toward his pallet. "I for one feel I have not slept in days. Let us take our rest. There will be more curious visitors tomorrow as word spreads. I feel like a prize ram on exhibit." He lay down and closed his eyes.

Martha and Mary could not help but stare down at him, reluctant to leave his side. Finally Lazarus opened one eye and looked up at their anxious faces.

"Don't worry," he grinned, "I shall still be with you in the morning."

19

Lazarus, who could not go about his usual chores without an audience of curious onlookers, was frustrated. People came up with small tasks of brickwork just to watch him. He flung up his hands, facing Martha. "How am I to go into Jerusalem now?"

Hanniel journeyed to Bethany as soon as he heard the news of the miracle and called on the family, embracing Lazarus with joy. Sherah was not with him.

To Martha's query he replied, "She has been ill and is forced to conserve her strength. She sends her love to all of you."

As they sat together to eat the evening meal, Lazarus pressed him for news.

"It does not look good," Hanniel said. "There is

word that the leaders have offered a ransom to anyone bringing them word of Jesus's whereabouts. They seek to arrest him."

Lazarus huffed. "Jesus called them 'whitewashed tombs' full of dead men's bones. They see but they are blind. They hear but they do not listen."

"Ah, that is a good description, my young friend, but they have the power and if they find Jesus, who knows what they will do."

Martha could no longer remain silent. She paused in serving and looked at Hanniel. "He taught in the Temple, in plain sight. If they were going to arrest him, why didn't they do it then?"

"They are afraid of the people. If they do anything at all, they will do it as secretly as possible."

Martha was adamant. "If the Master does not want to be found, they will not find him. I'd venture to say he will stay away from Jerusalem."

"Will he?" Hanniel stroked his beard. "The Scriptures talk of two Messiahs, one the conquering king, and the other a suffering one. Which one is he? Jesus has the support of the people right now and they would gladly crown him their king. What then of the Romans? Would they stand by and allow this? Would they consider it a rebellion against their puppet king, Herod? Pilate would call for more soldiers to protect his post and none of us would be safe from his retribution."

Lazarus stroked his beard, his brow furrowed.

"If what you say is true, what then can we do?"

"We can do nothing but wait." The old man's countenance was grieved as he turned to Lazarus. "I do not wish to bring sorrow on this house, but I bring other news. It concerns you, Lazarus."

Lazarus glanced at his sisters who hovered nearby, listening with growing alarm on their faces. "I believe I know what you wish to tell me. I have a friend who works in the household of Caiphas. They speak against me also, do they not?"

Hanniel nodded. "Many have believed in Jesus because of you. I do not believe there is immediate danger, but you must be careful if you come to Jerusalem. I will keep my ears open and warn you if I hear anything more."

Lazarus bowed his head. "I cannot go anywhere outside the house, let alone Jerusalem, without curious onlookers."

Martha thought of the rugs she wove that Lazarus sold in the marketplace for her. "If Lazarus cannot go into the marketplace, how then can he sell my weavings? That is part of our income."

Lazarus thought a moment. "Tobias. He would be glad to take them to the marketplace for us."

Hanniel shook his head. "Selling your sister's weavings is the least of your troubles, Lazarus. You are a curiosity to the people and a stumbling block to the Jewish leaders. You must be alert and watchful at all times."

That night, as the others slept, Martha lay awake, pondering Hanniel's words. Her world was changing rapidly and the unknown frightened her. Would the leaders seek to get rid of her brother? What choices did they have? Were they all in danger? Soft snores came from the pallets of Hanniel and Lazarus. At least they could sleep. She glanced over at Mary and in the dim light saw she was awake. Martha reached out a hand and Mary clasped it tightly with her own.

The next morning as Hanniel prepared to return to his home, Tobias and Nathan came by and the men went to the corner of the courtyard, speaking in low tones so Martha could not understand their words. She felt a growing alarm. What they were discussing was obviously not for her ears. She pursed her lips, determined to ask Lazarus about it later.

When Hanniel had gone, Lazarus went with Tobias and Nathan to Nathan's blacksmith shop. He was gone most of the day, and she assumed he was helping Nathan with some work. When he finally returned for the evening meal, she started to question him and received no response. Lazarus gave her a look that precluded any more questions. Was there some danger he was trying to keep from her? She bit her lip and said no more.

When she and Mary completed their duties, Martha quietly went up on the roof and fell to her knees to beseech the God Who Sees for the protection of her family. As the soft notes of Mary's lyre drifted up from the courtyard, in the gathering darkness Martha poured out her heart to the Lord.

20

Lazarus continued to keep a low profile and no longer went into the city. Nathan or Tobias took Martha's weavings into the marketplace and sold them for her. Lazarus worked their fields. The flax was harvested just after the Festival of Purim, and Martha viewed the approach of Passover with mixed emotions. Jesus said he would return to them six days before Passover. The family had word that Jesus was returning to Judea and was ministering near Jericho. As she thought of her cousin's words earlier that winter, she feared for Jesus's safety.

True to his word, Jesus approached Bethany just as he'd told Martha. She welcomed him and his disciples once again into their home.

Peter, usually opinionated, was silent, and some of the disciples wore worried looks on their faces. Judas Iscariot watched Jesus, but his face was a mask, and Martha wondered what he was thinking. John, James, Matthew, and the others spoke in low tones among themselves, and Martha noted that they glanced at the gate from time to time. Were they expecting trouble? Soldiers? She looked at the face of the Lord and saw sadness there, a sense of resignation. It puzzled her as she and Mary went about their tasks.

Knowing Jesus was there, a great many Jews came to Bethany, not only to see Jesus, but out of curiosity to also see Lazarus. Some of the Pharisees came also. They said little but observed Jesus and Lazarus with narrowed eyes. Martha was fearful of them and cautioned Mary to make every effort to be hospitable. She wanted no trouble at her home, and especially feared for Lazarus. She was aware through other women in the village that many in Bethany had believed in Jesus because of the miracle of raising Lazarus from the dead. Martha was glad for that, but she carefully observed the leaders as they listened to Jesus speak and felt their animosity toward him. With a start she realized that they were also watching Lazarus, and the look on their faces sent cold chills down her back. When they finally left, she was so relieved she nearly wept.

Mary passed her, carrying a bowl of fruit and, putting a gentle hand on Martha's arm, murmured, "I am glad they are gone too."

When at last it was just their family, Jesus, and his disciples, Jesus turned to Lazarus. "On the first day of the week I am entering Jerusalem. Will you join us?"

Martha paled as Lazarus spoke what they had all feared. "Master, it is dangerous to enter the city. The leaders plot against you. Did you not observe their manner when they were here?"

"We must all obey the commandment to observe Passover, my friend. Do not fear for me. I must continue to do my Father's will." He turned and looked in the direction of Jerusalem, and Martha was puzzled to once again see the sadness on his face.

News that Jesus was coming into Jerusalem traveled like lightning, and by the time Jesus and his disciples left Bethany, people came from all directions to follow them.

Martha pleaded with Lazarus not to go but, seeing he was determined, decided that she and Mary would go also. Surely there could be no harm done to Jesus with all the people around him.

Looking around her at the happy crowd, Martha forgot her fears and her heart lifted as she too joyfully followed Jesus and his disciples to Jerusalem. As they neared the Mount of Olives, Jesus stopped and called Peter and John to him.

"Go into the village opposite you; and as soon as you have entered it you will find a colt tied on which no one has sat. Loose it and bring it, and if anyone says to you, 'Why are you doing this?' say, 'The Lord has need of it,' and immediately he will send it here."

The group waited patiently as Peter and John hurried into the nearby town of Bethphage. People sat down on the grass of the hillside and waited. In a short time the disciples returned, leading a colt just as Jesus had said.

Some of the onlookers threw their cloaks on the back of the colt and Jesus sat on it. Then the people began to spread their clothes on the road while others cut leafy branches from the trees and spread them on the road in front of him. Women shook tambourines to add to the joyous sounds. Voices were raised in praise and Martha heard them cry out—

"Hosanna! Blessed is he who comes in the name of the Lord!"

"Blessed is the kingdom of our father David that comes in the name of the Lord!"

"Hosanna in the highest!"

Martha and Mary joined in the praise. Martha looked around her at the faces of the crowd. They were proclaiming Jesus the Messiah who has finally come, she thought to herself. How can they deny him now?

As the noisy procession descended from the Mount of Olives, some of the Pharisees called out to him from the crowd, "Teacher, rebuke your disciples."

Jesus answered them, "I tell you that if these should keep silent, the stones would immediately cry out."

As Jesus drew near the city he stopped and those near him, including Martha, saw tears rolling down his face. He looked toward the city, and as he spoke, her heart became fearful again.

"If you had known, even you, especially in this your day, the things that make for your peace! But now they are hidden from your eyes. For days will come upon you when your enemies will build an embankment around you, surround you and close you in on every side, and level you, and your children within you, to the ground, and they will not leave in you one stone upon another, because you did not know the time of your visitation."

Martha gasped at his words. When would this happen? She turned to Mary. "Did you hear what he said?"

"Yes, but I do not understand. Is the Lord speaking of a time to come soon or in the future?"

Lazarus, standing nearby, but careful not to stand with them lest he be recognized, spoke in a whisper from the cloak that hid his face. "I fear for him. I fear for all of us. He does not speak rashly. It is a prophecy."

With the exuberant crowd following him, Jesus entered the city, riding with his head held high as any king. The people followed him to the Temple, and to the people's surprise and delight, he once again drove out the moneychangers and those who bought and sold animals there. This was the second time Jesus had cleansed the

Temple. Martha remembered that first Passover, when Tobias and Lazarus had all but run from the Temple with their slain lamb, fearing the Temple police. Once again there was no action by the leaders, and when the bleating of the lambs and dust of feathers from released doves settled, Jesus began to teach. For some, the show was over. Many people who had not dispersed when the chaos began now began to slip away and the crowd thinned out. Those who remained listened attentively.

Martha stood with Mary behind one of the large pillars where Lazarus had drawn them once before for safety during the confusion. As Martha gazed over the crowd, she was puzzled to see Judas Iscariot glance at Jesus and the other disciples and quickly pull his cloak over his head as he slipped away by himself. He walked to the far side of the courtyard of the Temple and spoke briefly to one of the scribes. Then the two men left together. Judas was the treasurer for Jesus and the other disciples. Perhaps Jesus had instructed him to present a gift to the Temple. She turned back to listen to Jesus.

Jesus looked around at the faces of his listeners and began to tell the people a parable. "A certain man planted a vineyard, leased it to vinedressers, and went into a far country for a long time. Now at vintage time he sent a servant to the vinedressers, that they might give him some of the fruit of the vineyard. But the vinedressers beat him and sent him away empty-handed. Again he sent another servant; and they beat him also, treated him shamefully, and sent him away empty-handed. And again he sent a third; and they wounded him also and cast him out. Then the owner of the vineyard said, 'What shall I do? I will send my beloved son. Probably they will respect him when they see him.' But when the vinedressers saw him, they reasoned among themselves, saying, 'This is the heir. Come; let us kill him, that the inheritance may be ours. So they cast him out of the vineyard and killed him. Therefore what will the owner of the vineyard do to them? He will come and destroy those vinedressers and give the vineyard to others."

The people murmured among themselves and some cried out, "Certainly not!"

Then he looked at them and said, "What then is this that is written: 'The stone which the builders rejected has become the chief cornerstone'? Whoever falls on that stone will be broken; but on whomever it falls, it will grind him to powder."

A priest standing about ten feet from Martha curled his lip in disgust and turned to a fellow priest. "He speaks this parable against us. He continues to incite the people, this rabbi from the rabble."

Just then a servant came up to the first priest and whispered a message in his ear. The frown on the priest's face turned to a triumphant smile as he nodded. With one last glance back at Jesus, the two priests turned, and brushing people aside in their haste, went to the side door of the Temple.

The shadows lengthened and Martha needed to return home to prepare for the Teacher and those with him. The two women slipped through the crowd. Lazarus would wait a few moments and then leave separately.

Martha knew Jesus would come for the evening meal, and then possibly retreat to the Mount of Olives with his disciples for the night. She sensed he needed a quiet place away from the village.

Jesus and his disciples had come in separate small groups to attract less attention. They had covered their faces with their cloaks as Lazarus had done and left Jerusalem at dusk.

After supper was over, there was a knock at the gate and all eyes turned anxiously in that direction. Lazarus cautiously opened the gate and Simon entered the courtyard.

"Peace be upon this house."

Lazarus let out the breath he was holding. "Peace be upon you, Simon. Enter our home and welcome. We haven't seen you in several days."

"I have been preparing my household." Simon stepped into the house and stood near Jesus, who was reclining on a cushion at the table.

"Lord, do you remember saying that the next

time you were in Bethany you would be guests in my home?"

"Yes, Simon. I remember saying that."

"Will you come tomorrow evening after you have taught in the Temple?"

"Thank you, Simon. We will come." His eyes twinkled. "I'm sure Martha could use a respite from cooking so many large meals."

Simon turned to Lazarus. "You and your family are also welcome. Be my guests tomorrow."

"We would be glad to join you. Thank you for your kind invitation to my family."

Simon turned to go, but then stopped. "There may be a few people you don't wish to see. Two of the Pharisees are coming."

Jesus shook his head. "That is no matter, Simon. They are your guests also."

Simon clasped his hands together, and a smile spread across his face. "Thank you, Lord. My household will look forward to tomorrow."

Martha and Mary went early to see if there was any way they could be of help to Judith and Chloe. Mary had a wrapped bundle under her cloak, but Martha assumed it was something for the meal.

Evidently Simon's wife and daughter-in-law had been preparing the meal for days and Martha found she could just be a guest. She and Mary sat and were entertained by the chattering of

Simon's small granddaughter, Reza, now a beautiful child of three.

The two Pharisees, Elidad and Pedahel, arrived, and Elidad immediately looked for the best seats at the table but they were already taken by Jesus and Lazarus at Simon's request. The Pharisees took the seats indicated with reluctance, plainly considering them inferior.

Judith and Chloe had prepared dilled cucumbers with olives and goat cheese, squash with capers and mint, lamb and lentil stew with coriander, bread, fruit, fig cakes, and wine. It was indeed a feast and the disciples ate heartily as did Jesus and Lazarus.

Once, when Judith was putting another bowl of the stew on the table and removing the empty one, Martha, at another table, happened to look at Judas and observed him glancing warily at Elidad. When Judas turned to look her way, she occupied herself with the food on her plate and kept her face bland, as though she had not seen them. What did it mean? Did the men know Judas?

Just as the men finished their meal and were talking among themselves, Mary suddenly came and knelt at Jesus's feet. She was holding an alabaster flask. Martha's eyes widened. It was the flask of costly spikenard left over from the anointing of their brother Lazarus. So much had been donated by sorrowing friends and neighbors, they had saved the small amount left over in the storeroom. Before anyone could move or say anything, Mary poured the oil over the feet of Jesus. Then she began to wipe his feet with her hair. As the fragrance of the oil filled the house, the guests were too astonished to speak. Martha cringed in embarrassment, but before she could do anything to cover her sister's debasement of herself, Judas Iscariot spoke up, his voice dripping with scorn.

"Why was this fragrant oil wasted? It might have been sold for more than three hundred denarii and given to the poor."

Elidad and Pedahel also began to criticize Mary.

Jesus gave Judas a piercing gaze, silencing him, and the man sat back with a sullen look on his face.

Looking around the room, Jesus spoke sternly. "Let her alone. Why do you trouble her? She has done a good work for me. For you have the poor with you always, and whenever you wish you may do them good; but me you do not have always. She has done what she could. She has come beforehand to anoint my body for burial."

There was murmuring among the women, and the men appeared puzzled.

"Assuredly I say to you, wherever this gospel is preached in the whole world, what this woman has done will also be told as a memorial to her."

Their lips tight in disapproval, Elidad and Pedahel suddenly rose, thanked Simon curtly for the meal, and left. Before they went out the door,

Elidad gave Judas a hard look and followed Pedahel into the night. Martha glanced cautiously around at the disciples to see if they noticed Judas, but they were occupied with watching Mary. Once again, Martha shrugged off the uneasiness she felt around Judas. She was imagining things.

Mary was now sitting back on her heels, smiling up at Jesus, and he was speaking softly to her.

Martha sat perfectly still, her hands clasped in her lap. For once she didn't know what to do. Should she help Mary up? Should she leave them alone? To her relief, Thomas solved her dilemma. He got up and came around the table, reaching down to gently help Mary to her feet, his eyes alight with awe and love. Mary glanced at her brother, her eyes pleading with him to understand.

Martha held her breath and watched Lazarus. Would he rebuke her? She put a hand to her breast and waited. Lazarus sighed and said, "It's all right, Mary."

Thomas drew Mary to the far side of the courtyard and talked animatedly with her. Martha watched them and her frown deepened. Then her attention was distracted as she saw Jesus rise from the table. His disciples also stood.

"Thank you, Simon, for a fine meal."

"It was my pleasure, Lord. Thank you for gracing my humble home."

The disciples also murmured their thanks to Simon and began to walk toward the gate. Martha realized they would be returning to the Mount of Olives, perhaps to prepare for the Passover that began in two days.

As the disciples went on ahead, Thomas left Mary's side and waited by the gate as Jesus turned and did something unusual for a rabbi. He embraced first Lazarus, but then also Mary and Martha.

"Thank you for the hospitality you have shown me so many times over these last few years. Your home has been a haven for me after long hours on the road."

Simon raised his eyebrows at this display of affection between an unmarried man and woman. He cleared his throat, glancing at the two women.

"You and your disciples are welcome any time, Lord."

"Will we see you at the Passover celebration, Lord?" Martha asked, after regaining her composure.

Jesus gazed into the night in the direction of Jerusalem and she saw him lift his chin. "You will see me at Passover, my friends."

It was obvious that Thomas wished to speak to Lazarus, and Martha reluctantly went on ahead with Mary as Lazarus and Thomas walked slowly together, talking quietly. Martha tried to listen in spite of herself, but could not understand their words. She glanced at Mary, who also looked back from time to time.

Martha sighed heavily. She had a hunch she knew what the conversation was about. She also knew Lazarus would talk to her when they got home.

The men ended their conversation and Thomas caught up to Mary.

"I will see you again, as soon as it is possible."

He looked down at her face and Martha saw Mary's heart in her eyes. The love between the two young people was almost tangible.

"Goodbye, Thomas," Martha said pointedly, and seeing Martha's face, he nodded and, with a whispered "Goodbye," hurried to catch up to the other disciples.

When the three of them arrived at home, Lazarus asked Martha and Mary to join him in the court-yard. Mary's face was alight with anticipation.

"You spoke with Thomas, Lazarus?"

"I believe you know that, Mary." He cleared his throat and looked down at Mary's hopeful face. "Thomas has asked for my consent to make you his wife. I must confess I have not sought to arrange a marriage for you. So much has happened this last year."

Martha knew this was not unexpected, having observed Thomas and Mary together over these last months, but her mother instinct was strong. "What of Thomas, my brother? He has no home that we know of, no income. How would they live?"

Mary turned to her sister, her lovely face alight with love. "God will take care of us, Martha."

Lazarus appeared to choose his words carefully. "You are aware . . . Mary, that in the eyes of the elders of our village I am . . . uh, the male head of the household. You and Thomas may not marry without my consent."

Mary's face fell. "You will not give it, Lazarus?"

"Mary, I would be happy to give my consent, but your sister has a valid point. How and where would you live? Would you travel the road with the disciples like a common woman, sleeping on the ground, not knowing where your next meal is coming from? How could I face the elders if I allowed such a thing?"

"Many of the disciples are married, Lazarus, and Thomas has told me their wives travel with them from time to time. When they cannot go, they stay with relatives."

Martha sighed. "We have not seen any of the wives with the disciples when they have come here."

"They do not wish to place an additional burden on those who host Jesus and his disciples. Sometimes they stay together at the home of a friend or relative. There are many women who travel with Jesus. They help pay expenses out of their own means."

Martha's eyes widened. "Their means? How do these women earn money?"

"They sell goods, as you do, in the marketplace. They prepare meals on the road." Mary regarded her sister earnestly. "They are all good women, believers. One of Jesus's followers is Mary Magdalene, an older woman that Jesus cast seven devils out of. She is a widow who has an income from the business of her late husband. She buys them food and sometimes lodging in cold or rainy weather."

Lazarus stroked his beard thoughtfully. "You would agree to such a life, Mary?"

"I love him," she said simply.

Martha shook her head. "Love cannot enter into this, Mary." She looked meaningfully at her brother. "Must you make a decision right now? Could you not wait until Passover has ended, when you can speak with Thomas more fully on this matter? Would that not be wise?"

A smile tugged at the corners of his mouth. "Yes, Martha, that would be wise." He lifted Mary's chin with one finger. "I will speak with Thomas after Passover."

Mary clasped her hands. "Thank you, Lazarus, thank you."

Martha got up and began to do the evening chores. Mary hurried to help her. The two sisters did not speak, but Martha found Mary glancing at her from time to time. When their household was in order, Mary laid her pallet down and sank onto it. In a few moments, she was asleep.

Martha sat by Lazarus in the courtyard, the chill winds of winter cutting through her cloak. "What are you going to do?"

Lazarus sighed and studied his hands. "I don't know. I have no wish to break Mary's heart, but as you have pointed out, Thomas has nothing to offer her. I cannot let her go to live from hand to mouth on the road."

"Perhaps Thomas has assets we do not know about." In spite of her reservations about Thomas, Martha also had no desire to break her sister's heart. She deserved a home and children.

"True. Perhaps he has a home and family somewhere and would take her there."

Martha knew they were both trying to consider the positive aspects of Thomas's suit, but as they returned to the house and unrolled their own pallets, Martha wondered in her heart if they could let Mary do this. If Thomas was not the right choice for Mary, Lazarus must stand firm and seek another husband for Mary. Martha lay down and folded her arms. Yes, Lazarus must stand firm. She would make sure he did.

21

Martha, Mary, and Lazarus journeyed once again to Jerusalem for the solemn festival of Passover. Lazarus wore the dark cloak to make himself less noticeable in the crowd. He was still plagued by people who wanted to see him, and he hated being an object of curiosity.

Hanniel and Sherah welcomed them warmly as usual, but Martha could see that Sherah had little strength. Simon and his family went elsewhere this year. Martha had looked forward to seeing her friend Esther, but so far they had not appeared. She remembered Judith telling her that Esther was expecting another child. Perhaps she was unable to travel. Martha had hoped to share with the one friend she could be herself with. Disappointment weighed heavy on her spirit.

Word came to Mary from Thomas that Jesus and the disciples would celebrate Passover in a room that would be provided for them. Martha considered Mary's words about the women who helped Jesus and his disciples. Her thoughts tumbled about. Perhaps if she talked with Jesus after Passover about Thomas? She shook her head. That was not her place, it was her brother's. Surely he would talk with the Lord and find out more about Thomas.

Lazarus and Hanniel took their sacrificial lamb to the Temple and brought the slain animal back to be roasted. As the family waited for the lamb to roast, and the familiar dishes were placed on the table for the Passover meal, Martha struggled with the heaviness that weighed on her heart. Ever since Mary had anointed the feet of Jesus at Simon's home, she had a feeling of impending doom. Jesus spoke of his death. She couldn't believe that he meant actual death, but why would he have welcomed Mary's anointing with the spikenard?

Martha worked in a daze, the joy of Passover eluding her this year. So much had happened to their family.

Sherah came and laid a wrinkled hand on Martha's arm.

"You seem troubled, my dear. Can I be of help to you?"

Her kind eyes searched Martha's face, and Martha felt tears rise up and threaten to spill onto her cheeks. Sherah was a wise woman who had lived nearly sixty years. Martha suddenly felt the loss of her mother again and longed to talk to someone who would understand. As Sherah continued to smile up at her, Martha nodded her head slowly.

Sherah led the way into the house and shut the door. As they sat down on some cushions, the floodgates opened and all Martha's fears poured out as she unburdened her heart. She told Sherah of her fears for Lazarus, the heaviness she felt over Jesus and recent events, and finally, her concerns for Mary. They talked a long time and Martha felt a heaviness lift from her shoulders as she listened to Sherah.

"These are things for you to leave with God, Martha. You cannot stop the wheel of destiny from turning, and does he not know all things? He will show you what you are to do and what is best for Mary."

Martha nodded her head, listening quietly. She embraced the older woman and resolved to pray diligently to seek their God in the matters that troubled her.

The next morning Martha and her family rose to return home to Bethany. The Hillel had been sung at the stroke of midnight, ending the Passover ceremony. Martha felt better for having shared her concerns about Mary and Thomas with Sherah. The older woman's words rang in her ears. "This is a matter for God to handle, Martha. He will show you what to do." How hard it was for her to relinquish her concerns to God. She and her family had been the recipients of a great blessing, the friendship of Jesus, and the miracle of Lazarus restored to them. Why was it so difficult to trust? She had held the reins too long. As she said her morning prayers quietly, she gave her concerns to the God Who Sees, the one who had the answers she sought.

Sherah gave her a warm smile as they took their leave, and Martha smiled back, glad to have been able to talk with her.

As they journeyed through the city, Martha, Mary, and Lazarus looked around and at each other. There was a strange pall hanging over Jerusalem. People were hurrying to leave, but their faces were guarded, frightened.

Lazarus wrinkled his brow. "Something has happened." He turned to his sisters. "I'm going to talk with a few friends in the marketplace. I'll catch up with you later."

Martha started to protest, but Mary took her arm. "We must do as our brother has asked. It is not safe in the city. I have felt it all morning."

Spotting Simon and his family, Martha felt better about having someone to walk with on the journey back to Bethany.

Simon was not his usual robust self. He too seemed anxious to get his family out of the city as soon as possible.

"Simon, do you know what has happened?"

"No. So many rumors are flying around I don't know what the truth is. Someone told me that the soldiers finally caught up to Barabbas. He is in prison even as we speak."

"I will feel safer traveling, knowing he is no

longer in the hills." Suddenly she felt better. That must be it. "Lazarus has gone to talk with someone he knows. He will bring us word."

Simon shook his head. "These are dark times. I feel it in my bones. Let us hope that your brother can bring good news."

22

Hour after hour passed, but Lazarus did not come. Martha fought the panic threatening to overwhelm her. The chief priests wanted to get rid of Jesus, and remembering the warning of Hanniel, they also wanted to get rid of Lazarus. Was he in danger? Had he been found and arrested?

The two sisters busied themselves with daily tasks, stopping occasionally to glance toward the gate. Once they thought they heard the sound of his voice, and Martha rushed to the gate only to see it was a group of pilgrims. One of the men was shaking his head and murmuring to himself, echoing Simon's words, "These are dark days indeed, and now Barabbas."

Dark days they were. Barabbas was a robber and murderer. Why would people feel so frightened at his arrest?

She shook her head in exasperation. What was happening? Where was Lazarus?

Later that afternoon, exhausted by emotions as well as the heat that poured down in the courtyard, Martha and Mary sat on a shaded bench. Mary had prepared some fruit and cheese. They ate quietly; there seemed little to say. A lizard scurried across the hot earth and disappeared somewhere into the animal pens. It seemed the only movement. The animals were strangely quiet and huddled together. Little by little, Martha noticed the absence of sound around them. No cricket chirped; no birds sang in the sycamore tree. Martha turned to her sister, wondering if Mary sensed the same thing, when suddenly all around them the earth moved. The sycamore tree swayed and cracks appeared in the side of the house and the walls of the courtyard. Earthen pots of plants fell over and shattered. The bowl of fruit and cheese bounced out of Martha's lap and smashed on the earthen courtyard floor. The sky grew dark and menacing, hiding the sun.

Martha and Mary clutched each other in terror, and Mary cried out, "It's the end of the world!"

After what seemed like one long, terrible moment, the earthquake subsided. In the continuing darkness Martha stood unsteadily, still clutching Mary, who was weeping with fright. It was hard to see the house, let alone what destruction had occurred in the courtyard.

"Oh sister, what terrible thing has happened?"

"I don't know. I fear for Lazarus, wherever he

is. I hope he was not caught on the road when this happened." For Mary's sake as well as her own, Martha gathered her wits and took a deep breath. Putting Mary aside, she squared her shoulders. Someone had to keep a clear head in this household. "The earthquake is over; we must find a lamp."

Martha inched her way in the direction of the storeroom and felt around for an oil lamp. She found one and, holding it carefully against her chest, slowly moved back toward Mary, her sister's small whimpers of fright acting as a guide. Pausing to get a sense of direction, she saw the glowing coals of the cooking stove. She set the lamp down by the stove and reached for a twig. Touching its glowing end to the wick in the lamp, she held her breath and let it out with relief when the wick caught fire and began to burn.

"Come over here, Mary. We can sit by the stove for a while."

The two women sat down on the ground and held each other as they waited for the darkness to lift or the earth to move again.

In a few moments there was a knocking at the gate. To Martha's relief, she heard the voice of their neighbor Shaul calling to them. "Are you women all right?"

"We are all right."

Shaul opened the gate and held a lamp up. His wife, Helah, followed close behind him. "We knew

Lazarus was gone. How much damage is done?"

Martha stood up slowly as her neighbors picked their way carefully over the debris in the courtyard and came to stand by her. "I don't know. The house seems all right, but I'm afraid to go inside."

Helah put her arms around Martha and as Mary stood unsteadily, gathered her in also. "We will stay with you until the sun comes out again."

Martha looked skyward but there was nothing to see, not even a shadow across the sun. It was as if the entire world was one black, inky night.

Shaul spoke hesitantly. "I have seen this darkness in the middle of the day before, when I was a child. It lasted for perhaps half an hour and then the sun came out again. This is different. It didn't come on gradually and then fade away. It came suddenly with the earthquake. It is a sign of some terrible event, I'm sure. I pray the Lord of all the earth will have mercy on us." His eyes in the darkness glowed with fear over the light of the lamp, giving his face a haunted look.

Mary tried to compose herself. "What do you think this means?"

There was another knock and a voice at the gate. It was Nathan. At Martha's call, he opened the gate and entered. He was also carrying a lamp. When he saw the two sisters sitting by the cookstove with Shaul and Helah, he seemed visibly relieved.

"It is good that you were not in the house when

this occurred." He found a bench in the dim light and moved it over near the stove so the women could sit down on it. "The roof of my house caved in. I will need Lazarus's expert help to repair it."

"Stay with us, Nathan. Let me get something for us to eat."

He waved a hand. "Do not trouble yourself, let us wait until we have some daylight again."

Shaul moved over to stand by Nathan. "What do you think this means? It is very strange."

Nathan shook his head. "I don't know. I've never seen anything like this. When I was in Hebrew school, the rabbi told of an event like this, but it only lasted for a short time before the sun was visible again."

Shaul nodded sagely. "I was telling the women of a similar occurrence when I was a boy. Perhaps it is the same event."

There were sounds from the street, and women's cries along with muffled voices of other men.

Martha looked toward the gate. "I hope no one in the village was hurt."

The five of them sat quietly, their fear growing when the darkness did not lift. Both Nathan and Shaul tried to be strong for the women, but their faces in the lamplight belied their encouraging words.

It was a long time until at last the darkness began to lift. She wasn't sure how long it had lasted, but it seemed like hours. The thick clouds gradually gave way to sunlight again.

Nathan rose. "I must check my shop and see to the damage to my home." He gave a half smile. "Let me know when your brother has returned."

As he took his leave, she thanked him for his concern. Shaul and Helah also hurried away to assess the damage to their own home. Already Martha could see cracks in the walls of the court-yard and the house, but the house was intact. She sent a heartfelt prayer of thanks to the God Who Sees. Surely he had watched over them.

She turned to her sister. "It is over. We must clean up this mess before sundown when the Sabbath begins. I pray Lazarus will return in time for evening prayers."

Mary nodded. She was still trembling as the two women picked up pieces of pottery. Mary retrieved some earthen pots from the floor of the storeroom and gently placed the plants from the cracked vessels into the new ones. Martha swept the debris into a pile. She eyed the cracks in the walls. Lazarus would have to repair those. She paused and in her mind gave voice to her fears . . . if he returned to them.

Fear permeated the air. Martha could sense it. The whole village must be frightened. What did the earthquake and the heavy darkness mean? Her father, with all his stories, never mentioned such a catastrophe in his lifetime.

All over the village men were at work repairing

the damage from the earthquake. Two children had been injured slightly in one home, and one man had died of his injuries. In another home, a child had a broken leg; another woman in the village had been found under the rubble.

People gathered in small groups and talked in low tones of all that had happened. Some were still fearful of sleeping in their houses that night and many planned to sleep on the roof where they felt safer.

"Martha?"

She finally turned and saw Mary looking at her quizzically. "I called to you several times but you didn't hear me."

"Hmmm." Martha acknowledged her words.

"Is something wrong?"

"No. I was just thinking about some things."

Mary came closer and put a hand on her sister's arm. "We all have much to think about these days. I worry about Thomas, hoping he will send me word he's all right."

"I'm sure he will send word soon. He's probably busy fishing." Martha gave a wry smile. "A lot depends on how successful he is."

It was nearly the Sabbath, and the women hurried to prepare what they could. Martha wondered how many would travel into Jerusalem for the Sabbath services because of the earthquake.

Tobias came by and carried news that their home sustained some damage but felt it was fixable. Judith and his family were all right.

"I fear going into Jerusalem tomorrow. We do not know if another earthquake will strike. I don't think our house could stand another shaking like that. Many houses in the village are down. Some families have sustained injuries. It is said that Anna, the healer, has many to tend to." He paused. "Adah is dead. Part of the roof fell on her head. By the time someone found her, it was too late. Her neighbors are seeing to the body."

Martha clicked her tongue in sympathy. "Are there any others?"

"One man, old Jonas, but no other deaths that I know of yet. There are some injuries."

"Thank you for coming, Tobias. Send our greetings to your mother and family. I'm glad they are safe."

"I will. Would you let me know when Lazarus returns?"

"I'll send him to you." She looked around at the damage for a moment. "He may have some work to do here first."

Tobias nodded and went home.

Martha heated the lentil stew and banked the fire in the stone stove to retain the heat during Sabbath. She lit the Sabbath candles just before the shofar sounded in the distance signaling the beginning of the Sabbath. With a last glance toward the gate, she and Mary stood at the table. Martha put her shawl over her head, closed her eyes, and passed her hands over the flames of the candles, repeating the familiar prayer. In the absence of her brother, she wondered what to do about the part taken by the male head of the household. If he did not come, she and Mary would go into Jerusalem, despite the danger. She had to know what had happened to him. Surely Hanniel would be able to tell them something.

Suddenly the gate was jerked open and Martha's heart leaped as Lazarus stumbled into the court-yard, followed by Thomas. Their faces were drawn with pain and sorrow.

The sisters hurried toward them, and Martha spoke first. "What has happened? We were so worried for you."

Thomas turned to Mary and took her hands. "The Lord is dead."

She gave a cry and put her hand over her mouth. He helped her to a bench and sat with her.

Martha stood still in shock. "What do you mean, the Lord is dead? How can that be?"

Haltingly, his voice breaking at times, Lazarus poured forth the events that had happened in Jerusalem the night before and that morning . . .

"The Lord was arrested in the Garden of Gethsemane last night. Soldiers, armed with swords and clubs came with torches, led by that traitor, Judas Iscariot. We learned that he had taken a bribe of thirty pieces of silver to betray the Lord's whereabouts."

Martha gasped. "I knew something was happening. I felt it. When Jesus was teaching, I saw Judas leave the courtyard and go into the Temple with one of the scribes. I thought he was making an offering for Jesus and the disciples."

Her voice sounding small, Mary looked from Lazarus to Thomas and back and cried, "Did you not try to save him?"

Thomas hung his head. "To our everlasting shame, we ran. We deserted him when he needed us the most. We were afraid for our lives. One of the soldiers almost caught me, but I left my cloak in his hand and fled wearing only my loincloth." He began to weep. "I don't know where the others are right now. I hoped Lazarus was at the home of Hanniel and sought him there. They gave me a tunic and cloak to wear. We waited until morning and then made ourselves inconspicuous in the crowd that gathered in the streets."

Lazarus went on. "I sought to find out what was happening. We finally found John and learned from him that the Jewish leaders held a trial during the night at the home of Caiaphas. John knew someone in the household there who secretly let him in."

Lazarus pounded his fist into his palm. "A trial at night is against the very law they pretend to uphold, and in the home of Caiaphas, the high priest? Trials are to be held before the Sanhedrin in the council meeting place."

"They had already made the decision to find him guilty," Thomas added. "It was plain."

Tears ran down Mary's cheeks. "What happened after the trial?"

Lazarus bit his lip, holding back more tears. "They brought him to Pilate. To his credit, Pilate found no fault in him. Pilate wanted to let him go according to his custom to release a prisoner at Passover."

Martha wiped her own eyes with her mantle. "Pilate did not release him?"

Her brother's face hardened. "The people, no doubt urged on by the Jewish leaders, called for Pilate to release Barabbas . . . and crucify Jesus."

At the word "crucify," Mary cried out and began to slide from the bench. Thomas caught her and held her.

"Crucify?" Martha cried. "They crucified the Lord?"

Lazarus nodded. "They led our blessed Lord through the streets like a common criminal, carrying a heavy beam. They wouldn't even let his mother near him. His back was cut to ribbons from those terrible whips the soldiers use. He was bleeding so much I thought he would never even make it to Golgotha. The soldiers had pushed a crown of thorns on his head. Blood was dripping down his face."

Martha gasped, her heart pounding in her chest.

"They did that to Jesus? He was not guilty of a crime."

"No, sister, he wasn't, but I don't think that mattered to them."

Thomas spat out the words, "The only compassion those Roman devils showed him was to pull a man out of the crowd to carry the heavy beam for him when he was too weak to carry it anymore."

Martha swallowed and took a deep breath. "You saw him die?"

Thomas nodded. "We stayed in the shadows and watched until he cried out, and died."

"What did he say?" Mary held her fist to her mouth, her eyes wide.

Lazarus shook his head and seemed puzzled. "He said, 'Father, forgive them, for they know not what they do.' "

"Then he died?"

"Yes," said Thomas simply. "About the sixth hour. We were frightened, for the moment he died, the sky swirled with dark clouds and thunder. The earth shook violently and the clouds hid the sun. All those self-righteous fools who called for his death ran for their lives. People were crying out in terror."

Mary looked up with a start. "We felt the earthquake, just about that hour, didn't we, Martha? Shaul, Helah, and Nathan came to see if we were all right. The darkness stayed for such a long time."

"It was dark in Jerusalem also. People lit oil lamps and huddled in the streets. They were afraid to go inside the buildings lest there be another earthquake. As soon as the darkness lifted, Thomas and I hurried to Bethany to make sure you were all right."

Martha waved a hand at the courtyard. "You can look around to see the damage."

Lazarus noted the cracks in the walls and nodded. Then he turned back to his sisters. "There's more. You will not believe this, but I saw people walking in the city that I know were dead. Many were seen walking into Jerusalem. People were on their knees praying for God's mercy."

Mary looked from her brother to Thomas. "What does all this mean? What is to happen to us?"

Martha gasped. "People who were dead? Was it the same as it was for you?"

Thomas nodded.

"They just came out of the graves and walked into the city?" She sat down suddenly on a bench, trying to grasp the enormity of what he was telling them. "What is to become of us? What does this all mean?"

Lazarus sank down on the bench next to her and cradled his head in his hands. "I don't know . . . I don't know," he murmured.

"Where are the rest of the disciples now?"

Thomas shook his head. "I'm not sure. We just

scattered." He thought a moment. "I think they might have gathered in the upper room where we held the Passover meal. It is hidden away in a far part of the city. They might feel safe there."

Mary looked up, her eyes wide with fear. "But Judas was with you. He knows where the upper room is. Would he betray the rest of you?"

His eyes flashed. "I don't know. If he did, they will all be imprisoned. Let us hope his one act of betrayal was enough for him."

Martha thought of the sullen young man who had traveled with Jesus and observed the miracles. "How could he do such a thing to the one who had been his friend?"

Thomas let go of Mary's hand and stood. "I should try to find the other disciples. We need to strengthen each other at this time."

Martha thought of the city, full of Herod's soldiers. "Would it be safe for you to return?"

He nodded. "I'm sure I can slip into the city unnoticed. There are back streets I can use. The Jewish leaders wanted Jesus. I don't think they wish to arrest all the believers. Perhaps they will feel that now he is out of the way, we will all disperse."

Lazarus put a hand on his shoulder. "Stay with us for the Sabbath prayers, Thomas, it will comfort the women. Early on the Sabbath I will go into the city with you."

Thomas considered the request. "I'm not sure

we should travel into Jerusalem together. The Temple police might be looking for any of the Teacher's followers. Perhaps if I wait until the first day of the week, all might have quieted down." He looked earnestly into the face of his friend. "I would suggest you let me go alone. I fear you are more in jeopardy than I. I've heard the rumors. The Jewish leaders plot against you also. With Jesus gone, they feel the people will look to you."

"I wish no rebellion and I don't plan on gathering followers."

"You know that, but the Jewish leaders don't. You are still a threat to them."

Martha spoke urgently. "Please, stay here with us until we know more. We are frightened."

Lazarus stroked his beard thoughtfully and then, looking from Martha's face to Mary's, relented. "Very well, I don't wish to leave you unprotected."

The Sabbath prayers were spoken as Martha and Mary served the still warm stew and Lazarus said the prayer after their meal. They passed the Sabbath quietly. Reciting the familiar prayers brought a sense of peace to all of them. Since the family had always gone into Jerusalem for the Sabbath, their village being too small for a synagogue, it seemed strange to stay home. More than the fear of not celebrating the Sabbath properly was her fear for Lazarus. What were they to do?

They spent a quiet day, but Martha's heart was filled with anxiety as she watched her brother and his friend conferring quietly in the corner of the courtyard.

When at last they had their final meal of the day, and no Temple police had come, all was quiet. Martha lit the havdalah candle, signifying the end of Sabbath. Then the four looked up into the night sky at the three stars. The night was peaceful. A bird was singing a sweet song in the distance. So much had happened in only two days—it was almost like a bad dream from which they would all awake.

They laid out their pallets again with Lazarus and Thomas on one side of the room and the women on the other. They fell into exhausted sleep, weary in both mind and spirit.

The first day of the week, the women prepared a simple breakfast of bread and fruit. Lazarus prayed earnestly, not only thanking God for their blessings, but for Thomas as he returned to the city.

Mary filled a small traveling bag with food for him to take into Jerusalem—date cakes, two loaves of bread, and some cheese—but he did not leave until midday when the city would be quiet. He told Lazarus he would inquire of trusted believers as to the whereabouts of the other disciples.

Mary, her eyes bright with unshed tears, walked Thomas to the gate.

"Please take care, and don't take any chances. I hope you find the others and that they are safe."

He looked down at her, his eyes filled with love, and took her hand. "I will return when I can." He turned to Lazarus.

"If I cannot return right away, I will leave word with Hanniel. Somehow I will get word to you through one of the believers in the city. I don't know what awaits me in Jerusalem."

With one last sad smile for Mary and a nod to Martha and Lazarus, Thomas turned and, closing the gate behind him, started on the road to Jerusalem.

The small family went about the tasks of the day, but jumped at every sound outside in the street, still expecting the Temple police to burst into their courtyard any moment, seeking Lazarus.

Mary played on her lyre, soothing them all with her music, while Lazarus sat on a bench in the courtyard, staring at the gate. Martha realized he was deep in thought, but she dreaded any decision he was thinking of making. She busied herself sweeping but watched her brother covertly. When Lazarus finally stood up, her heart jumped.

"I have been thinking of Thomas's words and the words of Hanniel. It is not safe for me to stay here, sisters. It will only bring danger to you both. It would be better if I leave for a time."

Martha dropped her broom. "Leave? Where would you go?"

"Syria, possibly. I'm not sure. Anywhere outside Judea where the Jewish leaders can't get to me."

Mary put down the lyre and hurried to him. "Oh what are we to do? Can you not wait until Thomas brings word?"

He smiled at her, acknowledging her concern, but lifted his chin with determination. "I will wait three days. If I hear nothing from Thomas, I will assume the worst has happened and that I too must leave Judea."

Martha's mind whirled. Three days? It was a long time. Anything could happen in three days.

23

The first day of the week passed as did the second day. There was no word from Thomas. Tobias offered to go into Jerusalem and see if he could make some discreet inquiries. The family was grateful, knowing he was not someone the Temple police or the Romans were looking for.

Martha busied herself at her loom. Moving the shuttle and concentrating on the red, orange, soft blues, and cream of her yarns. She had watched the sunrise that morning and the vivid colors touched her heart. She pictured weaving the sunrise into the rug she worked on. Yet the intensity with which she worked didn't stop the questions that paraded through her mind.

Mary, preparing their bread for the day, kneaded the dough as though her life depended on it. Though each one found a way to occupy themselves, the time passed slowly. Lazarus took care of the animals, patched the wall in the courtyard, and began repairs to the cracks in their walls. Shaul and other men came to request his help on damage to their homes. To his relief, they treated him as they had before his miracle and it gave him some peace.

As the afternoon shadows lengthened and the air became cooler, Martha got up and went to get their water pot. Perhaps someone had brought news and the village well was the place to get it. She glanced at Mary, who raised her eyebrows in question.

"I'm going for water," Martha said, stating the obvious.

Mary's face reflected Martha's own anxiety, but she merely nodded and began to shape the dough into loaves.

Martha walked quickly down the road and saw that there were several women in a tight cluster at the well—Lea, Phoebe, and Judith. As she drew near, they made way for her, but Judith touched Martha on the arm, beaming broadly.

"I have just received news. Esther and Micah have another child, a girl this time. They have named her Sarah."

Martha smiled in return. It was good to hear happy news this day. "I'm glad for you, Judith, and for my friend, Esther. Will they be coming to Bethany any time soon?"

"Perhaps, when the baby is a little older and able to travel, but Simon and I have talked about perhaps journeying to see them in the next few weeks."

Women loved news of a new baby, and they spoke blessings on Esther and the new little one, exchanging stories of recent births in the village, how long the woman was in labor, and the topics that women who had experienced childbirth shared.

Though that news was good, the mood was somber. As Martha started to lower the water pot with the rope, one of the women stepped forward.

"You have heard the news about the Teacher?"

Martha paused. "Yes, I've heard. Lazarus told me that he is dead."

Judith shook her head slowly. "What a terrible death for someone who did so much good."

The women murmured among themselves.

Then Phoebe spoke up. "How will this affect our village? He came here many times. Would the leaders consider us dangerous?" She looked around at the group. "My Eli was there. He saw everything."

Martha bristled and out loud she said firmly, "Nonsense. Jesus stayed many places. They cannot arrest the whole country." Yet she felt the grip of fear on her heart. Would there be soldiers in their village? Would they arrest Lazarus? She drew herself up.

"We can only wait to see what happens." She looked around earnestly at each face. "We must pray for our families and our village at this time. The God Who Sees will keep us in his care." She spoke more bravely than she felt.

Lea looked at her. "But you had the Teacher in your home. Your brother's miracle is the talk of Jerusalem and our village. Are you not in danger?"

Martha just shook her head and occupied herself with drawing the water. Then she turned to the group. "The Teacher is dead. We had hopes, but there is nothing we can do now."

Judith's daughter-in-law, Chloe, who had been silent, spoke up. Since she was usually shy, the women all turned suddenly to listen. She looked at the group of women with wide eyes. "I have heard the men talking in the village. They thought Jesus was the Messiah, the one who would save us from the Romans. If he was truly the Messiah, he would have led a revolt against the Romans. He would not have allowed himself to be killed."

It was an impassioned speech for her, and the women listened with amazement.

Martha realized the girl was echoing her own thoughts and the thoughts of most of the village.

She could do nothing for Jesus now except be grateful the rest of her days for his teaching and especially for giving her brother back to them. She could always be thankful for those things the Master did while he was still alive.

The women spoke in hushed tones about the earthquake and friends who had remained in Jerusalem and saw the crucifixion.

A thought came to Martha and she turned to Phoebe.

"Phoebe, what can you tell us of the Master's last moments? You said your husband was there."

Phoebe stepped forward and lifted her chin, proud that she had important news to share.

"They crucified three that day, the Teacher and also two criminals, one on either side of him. There was only one of his disciples that Eli could see, the one called John. My husband saw him standing below the cross with the Teacher's mother. He said Jesus spoke to them from the cross, and John led the Teacher's mother away. Some of the women who traveled with Jesus and his disciples were at the cross also. That woman they call Mary Magdalene for one." Phoebe sneered in disdain. "His loyal disciples, with the exception of John, were nowhere around. It certainly didn't take much for them to fall away."

A retort rose to Martha's lips, but she thought better of it. Instead she gazed steadily at Phoebe. "They are in danger also. Would it not be wiser to remain out of sight instead of being in the open?"

Phoebe shrugged. "Then why was that one disciple there?"

Martha thought a moment. "I believe he is a relative of someone in the Sanhedrin. Perhaps the leaders were willing to overlook his association with Jesus."

The women nodded to each other. That made sense.

Martha had one last question. "What happened after John took the Teacher's mother away?"

Phoebe thought a moment. "I don't know. When the Teacher died and the earth began to shake, my husband ran with the others. Everyone was afraid. He just wanted to get home to make sure we were all safe."

Martha thought for a moment, then, "I wonder who took him down. It was the Sabbath. They would not leave him on the cross."

The women turned to Phoebe, but she shrugged and waved one hand. "How would I know? My Eli had already gone."

Talk about the death of Jesus cast a pall over the women's conversation. Suddenly they all had important things to do and hurried away to their homes.

Martha walked back home slowly, balancing the water jug on her shoulder. So many questions chased themselves around in her mind.

Who had come to claim the body? What had

happened to the disciples? Were they also arrested? Was Lazarus truly in danger? Would he have to run away to save his life? She didn't know a great deal more, but Tobias had gone into Jerusalem. Surely by now he would have returned with news. She quickened her steps.

24

Martha didn't realize how anxious she'd been until she felt the rush of relief to see Tobias talking with Lazarus and Mary. Her brother was shaking his head and as she approached, he turned to her with a strange look on his face.

"What is wrong? Has harm come to Thomas or the other disciples?"

Tobias spoke up. "I went into Jerusalem, to the house of your cousin, Hanniel, as Lazarus asked. Thomas sent a message with a trusted friend, who is a believer and also a scribe. After several discreet inquiries, Thomas found the disciples hiding in the upper room, as he suspected."

Mary cried out, "The upper room? That can't be a safe place. Judas could lead the soldiers there. Thomas could be arrested by now, with all the others."

Tobias shook his head. "Judas is dead. He thought that Jesus would rise up and lead a revolt when they arrested him. He'd said all along that Jesus should take his place as a leader of the people. I don't think he anticipated what would happen when the soldiers arrested Jesus. Judas was found hanging from a tree in the Potter's Field."

So Judas was dead. Martha realized that she understood what Judas had tried to do. He'd betrayed the Lord with a plan in mind, and it hadn't worked the way he wanted it to. Poor man, he must have been bitterly disillusioned to take his own life.

Lazarus waved a hand. "Go on, Tobias, tell Martha the rest of the story."

"Well, several of the women went to the tomb early the first day of the week, bringing spices to add to the wrappings around Jesus. Pilate had sent soldiers to guard the tomb and the great seal of Rome was placed on the stone at the entrance. They were worried about how to get in to anoint the body of the Lord. And this is the amazing part. Jesus was buried in the tomb of Joseph of Arimathea, who had gone to Pilate to request the body of Jesus."

Martha gasped. "He is a member of the High Council. He is a believer?"

Lazarus shrugged. "He must be. No one would have the courage to go to Pilate for that task."

Tobias went on. "The body was wrapped with some spices by Joseph and placed in the tomb quickly because the Sabbath was near." He paused as if his next words were more than he could speak. "When the women approached the tomb early on the first day of the week, they claimed that two shining beings had rolled the stone away and were sitting on the stone. These beings told the women that Jesus was not there, that he had . . . risen from the dead!"

Mary clutched at Tobias's sleeve. "Risen from the dead, just as he raised our brother?"

"Yes. The beings said, 'Come and see the place where the Lord lay. And go quickly and tell his disciples . . . and Peter, that he is risen from the dead and will go before you into Galilee; there you will see him as he said to you.' "

"Did they look in the tomb and see that Jesus was gone? And where were the soldiers?" Martha wanted something substantial to process in her mind.

"That's the strange part," Tobias said. "The soldiers were gone, every one of them."

"But they wouldn't leave their post," Lazarus murmured. "That is all very strange."

Lazarus took up the story. "Mary Magdalene along with the women returned to the upper room and she told the disciples she had seen Jesus and he had spoken to her. She'd thought he was the gardener and wanted to know what he'd done with the body of the Lord. Then she said he spoke to her, and when he said her name, she realized it was the Lord and fell at his feet. He told her not to cling to him as he had not yet ascended to his Father; but to go to his brethren and tell them he was ascending to his Father and their Father and to his God and their God."

Mary put an arm around her sister. "We must believe. If Jesus could raise Lazarus and others from the dead, could he not raise himself? Has he not told us he was going to the Father? We must consider the words he spoke when he was with us."

Martha sat down on a bench—it was almost too much to take in. "What did the disciples say when Mary Magdalene told them he was alive?"

Tobias snorted, "They didn't believe her. Thomas said John and Peter took off at a dead run for the tomb to see for themselves and came back mystified. The grave was indeed empty, and this is the strange part. The burial garments were still there, including the burial cloth which was lying on the stone slab." Tobias turned to Lazarus. "The cloth that covered his face was set aside by itself and neatly folded." He waited for the thought to penetrate.

His eyes widened and his mouth dropped open. "The tradition," Lazarus cried. "The master and his servant—we were taught that in school with the rabbi."

Mary looked from Lazarus to Tobias. "What tradition?" She sat down next to Lazarus on the bench and waited for Tobias to continue.

"Every Jewish boy knows the story. When a servant set the table for his master, he made sure that it was exactly the way the master wanted it. Then the servant would wait, just out of sight until the master had finished eating, and the servant would not dare touch that table, until the master was finished. Now if the master was done eating, he would rise from the table, wipe his fingers, his mouth, and clean his beard, and would wad up that napkin and toss it onto the table. The servant would then know to clear the table. For the wadded napkin meant, 'I'm done.' But if the master got up from the table, folded his napkin, and laid it beside his plate, the servant would not dare touch the table, because . . . the folded napkin meant, 'I'm coming back!' "

Tobias shrugged, embarrassed. "It is only a tradition and has to do with a napkin rather than a burial facecloth, but it came to mind when I heard this. I do not even know if the tradition is true. Perhaps it was just a story the rabbi told to keep the interest of squirming young boys."

Martha thought a moment. "I'm sure it has some significance, Tobias, or it wouldn't have come to your mind."

Her face alight with joy, Mary cried, "He is alive. I believe with all my heart that he is alive. We should rejoice that he came to us, and supped with us and caused us to observe the miracles so we would believe. Thomas told me once that Jesus said, 'I am the way and the truth and the life, and no man comes to the Father but through me.' " She clasped her hands. "Don't you see? He came so that we might believe, and because we believe in him, we too shall see the Father one day."

Lazarus nodded sagely. "I believe what you say is true. Our family has good reason to believe, for I am a living example of the resurrection from the dead."

He turned to Tobias again. "So what is next? How long will the disciples remain in the upper room?"

"I don't know the answer to that. We can only trust the Lord to show them what to do. Thomas said he would come to you sometime in the next two or three days and he'll know more at that time. He has not seen the Lord and was skeptical about the women's testimony, but I'm sure he will have further news when he comes."

After Tobias left them to return to his own home and share his glad tidings, Martha and Mary still sat on the bench. Martha tried to process the amazing news that Tobias had brought them. Finally, she rose and began making preparations for their evening meal. Mary sat for a moment longer, looking up at the clouds in the sky, her face radiating her joy. When Martha cleared her throat and gave her a stern look, she rose quickly and, taking the bread from the oven where it was wrapped in cloths, put it on the table and went to the storeroom for cups of water.

"I go to our God"—the words Thaddeus had said on the scroll. Jesus could not have done the miracles he did unless he was from God. Martha turned the words over and over in her mind as she moved about the stove and put platters on the table. Would she and her family see the Lord again? He had appeared to the women; surely he would come to the disciples and reveal himself again. He loved Lazarus as a brother. Would he not show himself to them? She thought of the picture of Mary Magdalene falling at Jesus's feet and actually seeing him and hearing his beloved voice. All of a sudden a great longing rose up in her heart.

25

It wasn't until the fifth day of the week that Thomas appeared at their gate. He came just after sunset and kept looking over his shoulder as if he might have been followed.

Martha had never seen Thomas so nervous. He usually had a ready laugh and an easygoing attitude. As he looked at Mary, his feelings were obvious. Had he braved any danger just to see her again?

"Peace be upon this house," he whispered.

Lazarus quickly shut the gate behind Thomas. Mary hurried from Thomas's side to prepare something for him to eat. The two men went inside the house where they could speak freely. As Martha put the warm lentil stew in front of him and Mary put down a half a loaf of bread and some figs, Thomas began to relax a bit.

The women waited patiently for him to satisfy his hunger, but Martha thought he'd never tell them his news.

Finally, Lazarus spoke up. "Tell me, Thomas, what have you seen in the city? What is happening?"

Thomas wiped his mouth on his sleeve and looked around at them. "I don't know what to believe of what I've heard. I'm sure Tobias told you that some of the women say they've seen the Lord. Then two of the disciples, Cleophas and Simon, who were traveling to Emmaus, told of a stranger joining them on the road. He asked why they were downcast and they told him of the crucifixion and that they felt all their hopes were shattered. The stranger began to expound on the Scriptures and tell of the things the Messiah was to suffer. He opened the Scriptures to them. They wanted to hear more and convinced him to turn aside at an inn with them for the night. As they sat at the table, eating, the stranger broke bread before them and to their astonishment, it was the

Lord! As soon as they recognized him, he disappeared, so they say, and the disciples hurried back to Jerusalem and the upper room to tell the others."

He absentmindedly broke a date cake in half as he stared out into the darkness. "The disciples even said, would you believe it, that he suddenly appeared to them in the upper room? Like a ghost, now he's here, now he's there." He hung his head. "I don't know what to think. It all seems part of someone's imagination. They wanted to see the Lord, so they thought they did. It seems like so many tall stories. They only make things worse."

Thomas spread his hands in a futile gesture. "I cannot just believe tall tales. Unless I put my hand in his side, and touch the nail prints in his hands and feet, I will not believe. The disciples wait in the upper room and no one knows what to do."

Mary sank down at the table on a cushion next to Thomas. "But, think of all the miracles we witnessed when he was here on earth with us; the blind healed, the lame walked, demons were cast out, and your own friend, our brother, was raised from the dead. Why can you not believe what he told us when he was here?"

Thomas gave Mary a sad, sweet smile. "I cannot plan the rest of my life on hearsay."

She sighed. "Will you go back to the upper room?"

His shoulders drooped. "Probably, I don't know what else to do. Peter and some of the others are talking about going back to Galilee to go fishing. I may go with them. I need to make some money. It's the only occupation I know."

He turned earnestly to Lazarus. "I want to show you that I'm worthy of Mary, that I can support her and make a home for her."

Lazarus stroked his beard. "Yes, my friend, I'm sure you do. I know this is a difficult time. All is not impossible." He leaned closer to Thomas and lowered his voice. "I must ask you to tell me if there is any further word concerning me and the leaders."

Thomas was instantly contrite. "Here I have thought only of myself and seeing Mary again. Of course you have waited for news. It is not good, Lazarus. Hanniel told me that double the number of guards watched the Sabbath services at the Temple. The Temple police also moved in and around the crowd. They didn't do anything, but they did seem to be watching for someone. I would not go into Jerusalem if I were you."

Martha huffed, "If they were looking for Lazarus, they know where we live. No one has come here from the Jewish leaders, no soldiers. It seems to me that if they wanted Lazarus, they would come here and arrest him."

Thomas shook his head. "You underestimate them. They didn't take Jesus in public because of the people that followed him. They took him at night in a secret place because Judas had betrayed him. If they want Lazarus, they will find a way to take him without attracting attention and quietly do away with him, lest they be blamed and there is blood on their hands."

Martha felt a cold chill go up her back and saw the fear on Mary's face.

Lazarus looked up at his sisters. "What can I do?"

"If I were you, I'd go away, Lazarus, until this all quiets down. When the leaders see that you are not starting a rebellion, it may be that they will discard their plans for you."

Mary put a hand on her brother's arm. "Perhaps Thomas is right. Maybe you only have to go away for a few months. They will forget about you."

He shook his head slowly. "It all seems too much to take in. My sisters would be left alone. They cannot tend the fields and do all the work themselves." He stroked his beard, deep in thought. Finally, "When will you return to Jerusalem?"

"I promised I'd come back on the first day of the week again. If the others are going fishing, I told Peter I would go with them."

Martha gave Thomas her warmest smile. "Then stay, Thomas, until after the Sabbath." In her heart she feared that Mary would not see Thomas again.

The two young people talked about marriage, and even Lazarus was moved by their devotion to one another. He agreed to give his consent to the marriage if Thomas could prove he could take care of Mary. The men talked about where Lazarus could go. Thomas confessed he had relatives in Damascus. If he had to leave also, there was a place he and Lazarus could go.

The morning after the Sabbath, Thomas once again prepared to return to the city. He'd made up his mind to go fishing with Peter and the others, determined to show Lazarus he could earn a living and support a wife.

Mary's eyes pooled with tears as she bade him goodbye once again and stood without moving, watching him trudge down the road to Jerusalem. The pain on Mary's face tugged at Martha's heart, and she went to put her arms around her sister and comfort her. For Mary's sake, she prayed that Thomas would come to no harm.

26

Nathan watched as Martha rolled up her two most recent weavings and bound them with a cord. He was going into Jerusalem and would take them to the rug merchant for her.

He picked up the bundles. "This is fine work. I should be able to sell them at a good price."

"Beware of Dothan. He is sly and will try to

give you next to nothing for them."

Nathan, no longer the taciturn man he'd been, grinned at her. "He will not best me, for I've traded with him before. You shall get a good price."

She smiled in spite of herself. "I'm sure I shall, Nathan."

When he had gone, she looked around the courtyard to see what needed to be done and checked the water in the sheep pen. A strange restlessness seemed to come over her lately. She tried to shake it off but found herself stopping in the middle of a task to look up at the clouds, or listen to a bird sing. Sometimes she would stand at the gate and look out at the sea of golden grain, waiting for the harvest.

Sometimes she imagined Jesus walking down the road to their house, laughing and talking with his disciples. What teaching they had heard. What miracles they had been privileged to observe. When she watched Lazarus working around their home, it was hard to believe he had actually died and been brought back to life.

The people had pinned all their hopes on Jesus, and when he didn't accept the role of their leader against the Romans, the fickle crowd had turned against him. Now the words of Thomas filled her with hope. Life would go on in their small village of Bethany as it had all these years before Jesus came. But she would never be the same. Her life would go on. Sometimes depressing thoughts assailed her, nothing new, nothing to look forward to. Just the endless cycle of woman's work: cooking, washing, baking. There would be no sound of children in their courtyard. Lazarus had more on his mind than marriage and anxiously waited for Tobias to return from Jerusalem. He was poised to flee at any moment, and many kept a lookout in the village to warn him of soldiers or anyone from the Temple approaching the village.

Mary touched her arm. "I'm going to visit with Chloe. Do you mind?"

Martha shook her head. "No, I don't mind. I'm going to cook the barley and lentil dish for tonight. Do we have any mint left?"

"Yes, there is still some growing in the shade in the garden. I'll get some for you."

Martha put a large pot on the clay stove and began to build up the fire. She poured some olive oil in and cut up an onion, moving it about until it started to brown. She added garlic, barley, and the lentils. Mary returned with the mint just as Martha was adding the lentils. She placed a clay platter over the top of the pot and let the pottage simmer.

When Mary had gone, Martha stood still, seeing her life passing by, always the same. She checked the pot, and after making sure it was simmering slowly, went into the house. Feeling like a foolish child who is getting into something she shouldn't, Martha looked around and then lifted the lid of the small chest in the corner of the house. She lifted the wedding dress a little and reached under it for the small scroll and medallion.

Clutching the medallion to her breast, she once again saw Thaddeus, waiting for her in the olive grove. She felt his strength as she had when she threw herself into his arms after her father died. She unrolled the small scroll and while she couldn't read the words, they were etched forever on her heart. She rolled it back up and placed it in the chest, then sat back on her heels, fingering the medallion. The love of Thaddeus had erased the rejection she'd felt when Phineas turned down her father's proposal. She had been loved, by a good man. Though it was but a memory, it was enough. She heard the gate open and quickly put the medallion back in its place and closed the lid.

She stepped out into the courtyard and greeted her brother. "How did it go today?"

"There is enough work to keep me busy for many weeks. I pray there will not be another earthquake to undo all my efforts."

He was making a joke, but as they looked at each other, the reality of the cause of the earthquake and the darkness played over in Martha's mind. The promised Messiah had died like a common criminal on a Roman cross. All the miracles he had performed couldn't save him from the angry crowd that had cried out for his blood. Like fickle children they had wanted him to do their bidding, and when he didn't they turned against him, urged on by the Jewish leaders.

Lazarus became thoughtful. "This is a strange day. I felt the need to come home sooner than I planned. I saw Mary coming from the house of Tobias."

"She went to visit Chloe."

A soft breeze began to blow in the patio just as Mary entered the courtyard. She had a strange look on her face. "I felt like I needed to come home. Is anything wrong?"

Suddenly a voice came to them, softly, as though brought by the wind. The voice was familiar.

"Thus it is written, and thus it was necessary for the Christ to suffer and to rise from the dead the third day, and that repentance and remission of sins should be preached in his name to all nations, beginning at Jerusalem. And you are witnesses of these things."

Martha looked about her, but there was no one else in the courtyard except the three of them.

"Did you hear anything, Lazarus?"

"Yes, I heard words, as though Jesus was speaking to me." He told her what he'd heard.

"Those are the words I heard!" Martha said.

Mary gasped. "I heard them also!"

He shook his head. "What is this strange thing? How can we hear the Lord speaking to us?"

"I would say it was the wind, or my imagination, but we all heard it. What can it mean?"

"I don't know, sister. I don't know."

She looked toward the Mount of Olives for a long moment, frowning, and then shrugged. She had no answers. They could only hope that Thomas would return from fishing with the other disciples, and bring them more information.

For the next three weeks, Lazarus continued working around the village, but by now his neighbors knew the danger he was in if the Jewish leaders decided to fulfill their threat. Watchers were casually posted as the eyes of the village watched the road to Jerusalem. He no longer went into the city for the Sabbath. He and the sisters quietly kept the Sabbath at home. Lazarus, just as a precaution, kept a traveling sack nearby, ready to slip away into the hills at a moment's notice.

Mary worked quietly, and many times Martha saw her smiling to herself. Perhaps she was thinking about Thomas.

Martha went about her tasks, yet several times had the strangest sensation that the Lord was nearby. It was as if he were looking over her shoulder and approving of what she did. At times it was so real she had turned, expecting to see him standing in their small courtyard. She could picture him sitting with the disciples, telling one of his stories. As she thought of him, a sense of peace washed over her. Maybe that is what he left with them, the remembrance of his presence, the memories of his words . . .

A joyful shout heralded the return of Thomas, and Mary's eyes shown brightly as she opened the gate. It was as if she knew the day of his coming and had been ready and waiting.

Martha and Lazarus rushed to greet him also.

The men embraced. "Thomas, what news have you brought us? Did you go fishing with Peter?"

Thomas grinned at them. "I have news that will seem unbelievable, and indeed, if I had not been there, I would be skeptical myself. The Lord lives."

Mary gave a glad cry. "I knew it. He has been with me these last days. I've heard his voice."

Martha glanced at her sister and frowned. "I know he lives in our hearts and memories, Thomas, but . . ."

He turned to her and shook his head. "No, Martha, he lives. He has returned from the dead as he said he would." Thomas motioned toward a bench. "Sit down and I will tell you what I've seen."

They sat, and Thomas began his story . . .

"When I returned to the upper room the second time after I left you, the disciples were excited and told me they had seen the Lord in his resurrected body. The doors were shut, locked, and he just appeared before them! Of course I thought they were just trying to impress me and didn't believe a word. I told them that I needed to touch the wounds in his hands and feet and put my hand in the wound in his side to believe." He flung up a hand. "I cannot believe I was so foolish." He went on. "Then on the next first day of the week, after I left you, I went to the upper room and I had not been there but a few moments, greeting my brethren, when suddenly, Jesus was in our midst." Thomas hung his head. "He said, 'Peace to you,' and he turned to me and said, 'Reach your finger here, and look at my hands; and reach your hand here, and put it into my side. Do not be unbelieving, but believing.'

"To my everlasting shame, he told me, 'Thomas, because you have seen me, you have believed. Blessed are those who have not seen and yet have believed.' "

"Praise God," Lazarus murmured. "Praise be to God."

"What happened next?" Martha asked breath-lessly, soaking in Thomas's words.

Thomas waved a hand. "We went fishing."

Lazarus frowned. "Fishing? After the Lord appeared to you?"

"Yes, my friend. For he vanished again, and after several hours, Peter announced he was going fishing and we looked around at each other, not knowing what to do, and several of us got up and left with Peter." Thomas flashed his grin again. "We did well."

This was something Lazarus could identify with. "How many fish did you catch?"

"We fished all night and in the morning had caught nothing. Then we saw a figure on the beach. He said, 'Children, have you any food?' and we answered, 'No.' Then he told us to cast the net on the right side of the boat and we would find some. We did, and suddenly we could hardly draw the net for the abundance of fish. John looked back at the beach and cried out, 'It is the Lord!' "

Mary looked at Thomas, her face alight with joy. "He appeared to you again."

"Yes. Peter jumped into the sea and swam to shore and the rest of us rowed the boat, for we could hardly drag the net for all the fish. When we got to the shore, there was a fire of coals and some fish laid on it, and bread." He turned to Mary. "He actually ate with us."

Martha was still puzzled. "How could he actually eat? He was dead and then alive, but he actually ate with you?"

"Yes. He was showing us his resurrected body." Thomas shrugged. "I don't understand it all, but I believe."

Then, to Martha's surprise and delight, the joy began to rise up in her soul. The Lord was alive again. He had said he would rise again, but she hadn't understood. Now she knew in her heart that the words Thomas spoke to them were true.

The Lord was alive. She leaned her head back against the house and let the joy flow through her, cleansing, refreshing joy, washing all the doubts away.

Lazarus turned to a more practical thought. "You said you did well with the large cache of fish . . . ?"

Thomas reached into his sash and produced a good-sized bag of coins. "This is my share, enough to provide for, ah, many things." He glanced at Mary, who blushed, and looked pointedly at Lazarus.

Lazarus let out a bellow of laughter. "Point well taken, my friend." Lazarus turned to Mary and Martha, and with an arched eyebrow asked, "Are you up to planning a wedding?"

Mary hugged her brother. "Oh Lazarus, thank you, for both of us."

Thomas then took her hands as they looked into each other's eyes.

Martha stood up and smiled gently at her sister. "You should have a proper wedding, Mary, but it appears there is no time." She turned to her brother. "Lazarus, do you think Tobias will go into Jerusalem to secure a rabbi to perform the ceremony?"

He nodded. "I'm sure he will go for us. You realize, sister, that we cannot invite the whole village. It would draw too much attention."

Mary stepped forward. "Surely we can trust

Simon and his family, and our neighbor Shaul and his family."

Her brother stroked his beard a moment and then agreed. "We must invite Nathan also. He has been a good friend to us."

Martha looked around the courtyard, considering what needed to be done. "We'd better get busy."

Lazarus slipped out and soon returned with Tobias and Nathan. The three men put their heads together. The problem was getting a rabbi. Perhaps they would let him think he was just marrying two young people from the village.

Nathan snorted. "If enough silver crosses the rabbi's palm, he will perform the marriage and keep his silence."

Thomas murmured, "I don't think I'm in danger. He may not recognize me as a disciple." He turned to Lazarus. "It is you, my friend, he may recognize. We must take a chance on the rabbi."

Martha sighed heavily. "All this secrecy will be the death of me."

They were all silent for a moment and then Mary asked in a soft voice, "Thomas, do you think the Lord will appear to you again?"

He shrugged. "He comes and goes as he pleases, but yes, I believe he will show himself to us again. I just don't know when."

Tobias agreed to go into Jerusalem and procure a rabbi for a small wedding in Bethany. Perhaps thinking of another hasty wedding, he smiled at them. "I know just the man for the task."

Judith and Chloe came quietly to the house with Chloe's small daughter, Reza, bringing date cakes and some fruit. They also brought a canopy that Tobias and Chloe had used for their wedding. It had been rolled up and put in their storeroom. Mary slipped next door and told Shaul and his wife, Helah. They came quickly and Helah brought some fresh-baked bread and some wine. The women prepared what they could, but it would be a meager wedding supper by Martha's standards.

Nathan, Tobias, and Shaul would hold the canopy, but there was a problem. They needed a fourth man. After much whispered discussion, Nathan went to get his elderly neighbor, Joseph. The man was hard of hearing, and would probably not understand all that was going on, but in this situation that was an advantage. Nathan felt he could be trusted to keep the matter quiet.

Martha, Judith, Helah, and Chloe took Mary into the house. Reza was told to sit quietly on a cushion, and she watched with wide eyes, holding the doll Martha and Mary had given her during the Feast of Lights.

Martha opened the small chest and lifted out her mother's wedding dress. "If anyone is to wear this, sister, I am glad it is to be you."

Mary removed her shift and the dress was slipped over her head. Mary would have to wear her best sandals, for there was no time to buy any new ones for the wedding.

Judith brushed Mary's hair to a shine and from her bag produced the blue shawl that Martha had made for her daughter Esther at her marriage. Martha's eyes widened.

"I'd forgotten about that." She gave Judith a puzzled look.

"The last time Esther was here, there was so much going on, she accidentally left it behind. I meant to return it to her the next time she came, but with the new baby, she has been unable to travel. I'm sure she would be pleased to have Mary wear it for her wedding." She smiled at Martha as she held it out. "Perhaps the God Who Sees knew it would be needed."

The soft cloth was draped over Mary's head and shoulders, and to Martha it seemed the perfect touch. Mary was ready—now all that remained was to wait for the rabbi and Tobias to arrive.

Martha stood before her sister with a touch of sadness. Now she knew what Shua's parents felt when they had to be party to a hasty wedding because of Tekoa.

"I had envisioned more for you than this on the day of your wedding."

Mary smiled up at her, her eyes bright with excitement. "Do not grieve, Martha. I am happy to be marrying my Thomas. Whatever the future holds, we can face it together. It is a joyous day for me."

Martha nodded and embraced her sister briefly. "I know."

As time passed, she was beginning to be concerned. What if Tobias was unable to get a rabbi to come with him? It was not the Sabbath, it was the middle of the week. Surely there was someone who was available.

It was nearly two hours later that Tobias arrived, and he had a rabbi with him. Martha came from the house and felt alarm rise. She had never seen this rabbi before.

Tobias introduced the man to the group as Rabbi Hezekiah. "He is a friend of your cousin, Hanniel," he told the uneasy assembly, then grinned. "He is also a believer."

Tobias had gone to the house of Hanniel and Sherah with his dilemma, and after listening to what was needed, Hanniel had gone to the Temple and come back with Hezekiah.

Thomas, who had been waiting uneasily in a corner of the courtyard, came forward. The canopy was opened and held by the four men, and Lazarus led his sister from the house to meet her bridegroom.

The ceremony was simple, but with gentle and profound words, Hezekiah entrusted Mary to Thomas and their vows were sealed. Martha watched with tears in her eyes. She felt as if she were giving a daughter away. As the young couple said their vows, for a moment Martha pictured herself standing under the canopy . . . taking the hand of Thaddeus . . . She shook her head and willed the thoughts away. She wiped her eyes. Her tears should be happy ones for her sister, not for the past.

As the guests partook of the food and wine, it was a subdued group. Martha saw the rabbi take Lazarus aside and murmur a few words to him. Lazarus hung his head a moment and then nodded. The rabbi clasped him on the shoulder and then turned to the guests.

"I thank you all for making me a part of your celebration. May the bride and groom have many years together and serve our cause with all their hearts. I must return to Jerusalem at once." He blessed them and turned toward the gate. When he had gone, Nathan and Lazarus came to Martha.

"Sister, the rabbi gave me a word of warning. The High Council is meeting tonight. Evidently I am the subject of their meeting. The rabbi said that someone will come and bring me word of their decision. I fear it will not be good."

Martha put a hand to her breast. "Oh Lazarus. Has it come to that at last?"

Nathan glanced at the newly wed couple and murmured, "Let us not spoil their day. There will be time enough when Mary must be told."

The celebration was brief, and the guests slipped away to their homes early as if they had just been visiting and supped with the family. The wedding dress was placed carefully back in the small chest, and Mary put on her shift again. For their wedding night, Thomas and Mary were given the room they had kept prepared for Jesus when he was able to come to Bethany. The Lord would not use it again, Martha realized with a sigh.

Nathan prepared to leave also and turned toward Martha. He seemed to want to say something to her, but finally wished Thomas and Mary blessings on their marriage, and with a brief hand on the shoulder of Lazarus, he gave her one last long look and then left for his own home.

Martha watched him go and stifled her curiosity. A strange man, Nathan. A good friend to their family, but she had long since given up trying to understand him.

27

The next morning Martha woke with a sense of expectancy. She wasn't sure why, but as the sun broke upon the horizon, she listened to the sounds of the birds and the bleating of their five sheep. With the warmth of the month of Shebat, the almond trees were in blossom and she and

Lazarus had slept out in the courtyard to give Mary and Thomas more privacy.

She looked toward the animal pens. Their female goat was due to deliver a kid anytime now. Then she saw her brother's pallet. It was rolled up already and there was no sign of Lazarus. Anxiety filled her. Had he gone somewhere in the middle of the night?

The gate creaked, and as Lazarus entered the courtyard, she breathed a sigh of relief. "Where were you?"

He gave her a wan smile. "I went to check the fields. The flax is doing well."

Martha began the task of making the bread, and when it was rising, she prepared some fruit and cheese for their breakfast. There was no sign of Mary and Thomas yet, and she shrugged to herself. If they could not sleep late on this morning, when could they? They had much to face in the coming days and weeks.

Suddenly the bridal couple appeared and their faces were radiant. Before they could speak, Martha heard a familiar voice in her head. She turned to Lazarus and from the look on his face, realized he was hearing it also.

Before Martha could speak, Lazarus murmured, "Go to the Mount of Olives."

Martha nodded. "Yes, the Mount of Olives. Did you both hear what I heard?"

The newlyweds nodded. "He has spoken

to us. We're to go there, now."

Lazarus covered himself with his cloak. Martha banked the fire and set the pot aside. Then the two women grabbed their shawls, covering their heads as they followed their brother and Thomas through the gate.

They walked quickly, savoring the freshness of the morning. The olive trees were bathed in the soft light of the rising sun, and as they passed into the trees, they were greeted by a sight so amazing they fell to their knees.

The ten remaining disciples were gathered, along with a small group of women, and in the middle of the group, smiling at them, stood Jesus.

With tears streaming down her cheeks, Mary cried out, "My Lord!"

Lazarus gave a glad cry of joy. "Master!"

Mary's face radiated her devotion as she knelt before Jesus.

Thomas came forward and gently lifted Mary to her feet as they beheld the one they thought they'd lost forever.

Forgive me, Lord, Martha cried in her heart and felt the peace as he gazed at her with love. Nevermore would she carry any doubts.

Martha stood and hesitantly moved toward Jesus. He held one hand out to her and she touched his wound. Then Jesus turned to face those who had assembled there.

"These are the words which I spoke to you while

I was still with you, that all things must be fulfilled which were written in the law of Moses and the Prophets, and the Psalms concerning me. Thus it is written, and thus it was necessary for the Christ to suffer and to rise from the dead the third day, and that repentance and remission of sins should be preached in his name to all nations, beginning at Jerusalem. And you are witnesses of these things. Behold, I send the Promise of my Father upon you; but tarry in Jerusalem until you are endued with power from on high."

He shared Scriptures with them that opened their understanding, and Martha listened intently with the others.

"It is not for you to know times and seasons, which the Father has put in his own authority, but you shall receive power when the Holy Spirit has come upon you; and you shall be witnesses to me in Jerusalem, and in all Judea and Samaria, and to the end of the earth."

With one voice, those assembled cried out, "Yes, Lord."

Then, as they watched, Jesus's clothing took on an iridescent glow and he began to rise into the air, disappearing in a cloud that had formed over them in the shape of a man's hand.

Martha stood next to Lazarus, her eyes wide and mouth open. Mary and Thomas held each other and no one spoke. They stood watching the sky where Jesus had gone. Suddenly two shining beings in white materialized in their midst.

"Men of Galilee, why do you stand gazing up into heaven? This same Jesus, who was taken up from you into heaven, will so come in like manner as you saw him go into heaven." Then the shining beings disappeared.

The group stood still for a long moment and finally looked around at each other, sharing their amazement at what they had been privileged to see.

Peter broke the silence. "He told us to wait in Jerusalem until the Holy Spirit comes. Let us return to the upper room and wait as we've been told."

The others nodded assent and began walking back to the city.

Mary turned to Lazarus and Martha. "I am going with Thomas to the upper room. Together we will wait for the promised Holy Spirit."

Martha saw conflicting emotions on the face of her brother. Torn between wanting to join them and the danger of entering the city. Then Lazarus was aware of John standing nearby, wanting to speak to him.

"Lazarus, as you know I have a friend who works in the house of Caiaphas. Some of the religious leaders met there last night. They are plotting your death and how to take you secretly. Your life is in danger."

Lazarus shook his head sadly, his shoulders

drooping. "Thank you, my friend, for the warning. I thought that after a week or so the furor would die down, but evidently it hasn't."

John put his hand on Lazarus's shoulder. "I wish there were more I could do. I'm sorry." He dropped his hand and turned to catch up with the other disciples.

Lazarus turned to Thomas and his sisters and shared what he'd been told.

Martha took a deep breath. "We will manage, Lazarus. Your safety is more important. Let us quickly return to our home and gather some provisions for you."

"Remember that I told you I have relatives in Damascus?" Thomas picked up a stick and sketched a simple map in the dirt. "I will send greetings with you and they will welcome you into their home as they would welcome me. Jesus healed my aunt of a continuing disease. They are believers."

"Thank you, Thomas, for your kindness." He looked down at Mary's face, her eyes full of hope. "Go with Thomas. He will take care of you now."

Mary clasped her hands and her eyes filled with tears. "Thank you, Lazarus. Thank you. I pray you might be able to return soon."

Martha hugged her sister and gave Thomas a stern look. "I also trust you to take care of my sister and protect her."

"I will honor her. You have my word."

The two sisters embraced again and wept briefly together. Then the young couple turned toward Jerusalem.

"Let us waste no time, sister." Lazarus was already striding toward Bethany and Martha could barely keep up with him. As they approached their house, Lazarus looked in every direction for signs of soldiers or the Temple police, but all appeared quiet.

Martha grabbed date cakes, fruit, a loaf of bread, some nuts, and a goatskin bag. She filled the bag with water, while Lazarus packed a change of clothing and a few necessary things he rolled up with a cord to sling over his back. He went to the small stone crock in the storage room where he kept what money they had.

"Take it all, Lazarus. You'll need it. Nathan will take my last weavings into Jerusalem. I'll be all right."

He hesitated and then embraced her. "You have been more than a sister to me, the only mother I have known in many years. I don't even remember our real mother. I want you to know how much I appreciate all you've done for me."

Martha blushed and then waved a hand. "Don't waste any more time, Lazarus. You aren't out of danger yet. You can make speeches when you return."

She smiled bravely as he turned back to wave at her and then watched him walk down the road.

He would have to avoid Jerusalem and there might be danger in the wilderness between Jerusalem and Damascus. "O God Who Sees, watch over Lazarus and keep him safe," she whispered.

When his tall figure became but a speck in the distance, she reluctantly turned and entered the courtyard. It was quiet, too quiet. Mary's lyre lay on a bench and Martha wondered if she would ever hear Mary play it again.

The animals became restless, and she realized it was their feeding time. Lazarus usually took care of the animals. Now it would be her job. She stared at the small pottery stove. She should cook something, but who was there to cook for now except herself?

She fed the animals and milked the goat, pouring the liquid into a stone storage crock. It was time to make goat cheese again. Would Mary be back to help her? She sighed heavily. Nothing was certain at this time.

She swept the patio and thought about turning to her loom to finish the shawl she was making, but instead sat down on the wooden bench in the shade.

Had it been a dream—seeing Jesus? What an amazing privilege she and her family had been given, to host the Messiah and his followers. In her mind's eyes she still saw them scattered about the courtyard in groups, talking, laughing, and relaxing from their travels on the road. She pictured Judas with his handsome face made less handsome by the frown that he continually wore. A strange, misguided man.

And Jesus. Here in this courtyard he had rested, told his stories, and touched people's lives forever. She relived the moment when Lazarus, bound in grave clothes, had stumbled forth from the tomb, brought back to life when Jesus commanded him to come forth. She thought of Simon and the miracle of his cleansing from the death sentence of leprosy. Had not very God visited them here on earth?

She wondered how many in Bethany had seen the cloud in the form of a man's hand, like a benediction, hover over Mount Olivet, waiting to receive the Lord as he rose out of their sight. She would no doubt have to field questions when she went for water.

Then there was Mary and Thomas. She knew now that they were meant to be together and had the Lord's blessing, as well as that of her brother. How brave they were, going off into an uncertain future.

Gradually a thought worked its way into her subconscious. She didn't want to think about it, but she could no longer deny the truth. She was alone. Lazarus was gone, for all intents and purposes. Mary was gone. All her life she had managed things, yet had Mary and Lazarus to help do their share. Alone. The woeful sound of the word that slipped out suddenly filled her with apprehension. What was she to do now? Could she handle the fields, the olive grove, the fig trees by herself? No, but she was sure she could get neighbors to help her with those things. She would have to pay wages for some of the work or pay them in kind. It was here that she felt it the most; no one at her dinner table to serve, just her and the animals. Her face became flushed with heat and tears pooled in her eyes. She didn't want to be the strong one anymore. She wanted someone to help share the burden.

She rose and looked around for something else to do. She could make some barley gruel. It would last her for a couple of days. Determined not to feel sorry for herself, she went to the storeroom and gathered some cloves, barley, some lentils, and an onion. She had no meat until she went to the marketplace. It would be fine without meat.

As the gruel was cooking, she wondered if Nathan had returned from the city and had been able to sell her rugs. She needed supplies and she'd given all the coins to Lazarus.

As the day waned into sunset and then twilight, she realized Nathan was not going to come, at least not today, and busied herself with cleaning her platter and banking the fire for the next day's cooking.

When the sun finally set, she stood a long time, looking at the emerging starry sky. She prayed for Lazarus, wondering where he was spending this night and how far he had gotten. He'd promised to send word back to her when he arrived in Damascus, but she didn't know how long it would take to get there. Had he made it safely past Jerusalem? Had he found a caravan to travel with? She could only wait and pray.

She thought of Mary and Thomas. There would be other women in the upper room to watch over her, Thomas had promised. Mary Magdalene, Mary, the mother of the Lord, and the wives of other disciples. She wasn't sure what the Lord had told them to wait for, only "tarry until they were given power from on high." What kind of power did the Lord mean? She remembered that when the Lord had sent the twelve out to minister in his name, they had come back rejoicing at the miracles that had happened. Thomas had told Mary of many people healed, just because they prayed in the name of Jesus. What move of God was happening in the upper room? No doubt Mary and Thomas would be back to share with her.

A cricket chirped by the house. It was a cheery sound as she checked the animals and secured the gate. The animals moved in their pens as they settled down for the night. She stroked the soft muzzle of the donkey, and as he nuzzled her hand, she felt he missed the one who usually fed him too. She studied the she-goat with her bloated stomach. The kid would come soon. She must keep an eye on the mother, she thought, remembering a time when a kid was trying to be born and it was breech. She had used her slender hands and arms to turn the baby around and it had been born healthy. Her father had praised her highly for what she'd done and she'd basked in his praise.

She secured the door of the house, but as she put the bar in place, she realized how seldom they had actually used it when Lazarus was there. Long after the lamp had been blown out, she lay in the darkness and listened to the owl call to his mate. It seemed to her a haunting sound.

28

The next morning she rose quickly, surprised that she had actually slept. She thanked the God Who Sees for watching over her and added her morning prayers. She had just bound up her hair when there was a knock at the gate and she heard a familiar voice.

She hurried to unlock the gate. "Good morning, Nathan."

He stepped hesitantly just inside the gate and glanced around the courtyard.

"Is anyone else here?"

"Mary has gone to Jerusalem with Thomas . . ."

He frowned. "There is danger in the city for all the disciples." He shrugged. "But they are married. She must go with him."

"Nathan, Lazarus has gone."

"Gone? Where?" The big man's face registered his confusion.

She smiled at him then. "Yesterday was a very eventful day, one I can hardly believe myself."

He stood, awkwardly, surely aware that he, a single man, was alone with a single woman in her courtyard. Before he could protest, or make his escape, she began to tell him what had happened . . .

"He left for Damascus yesterday. John told him the High Council was arranging for his death. He had no choice. Thomas has relatives in Damascus. They are believers and he urged my brother to go there for safety."

His shoulders sagged. "I hoped the rumors were not true." He glanced at the gate, appearing ready to step out should a neighbor pass by.

He looked back at her. "I have heard other news, of strange sightings in the city and that Jesus is alive . . . that others have seen him."

"Oh Nathan, if only you could have been there. He called the four of us to the Mount of Olives . . . it was as if we heard the words in our heads. We went there and there he was."

"Jesus?"

"The Lord and Messiah. The disciples were

with him and his clothes, Nathan, it was as if they shone like the sun."

His face was suddenly eager. "You saw him then?"

"Yes. He told the disciples to wait in Jerusalem until they received some sort of power from on high, and then he just rose in the air."

"Like a ghost?"

She smiled. "No. He was not some apparition. He showed us the nail prints in his hands and feet. He let me put my finger in the wounds of his hands."

"How did he rise up in the air?"

"There was a cloud, in the shape of a man's hand above him. He just left the ground and entered into the cloud and was gone."

Nathan's face registered astonishment, then his shoulders sagged. "I would have liked to have been there."

She felt his disappointment and went on quickly. "He said the disciples would receive power when the Holy Spirit came upon them and that they shall be witnesses for the Lord in Jerusalem and in all Judea and Samaria, and to the end of the earth."

"Did he say he would return?"

She shook her head in wonderment. "Oh yes, Nathan. We were standing there, looking up into the heavens when two men in white apparel suddenly stood by us. They said that this same Jesus who was taken up into heaven, will come again in the same way."

Nathan digested her words solemnly. "Then we must do as he has told us." He stood for a long moment, contemplating the words of Jesus. Then all of a sudden, he seemed to remember that they were alone. He backed hastily out of the gate.

"I'm sure your sister and Thomas will return soon. Is there, uh, anything you need?"

"I'm going to be all right, Nathan." She resisted a smile. He was ready to bolt. "I will have more rugs to sell in Jerusalem in a day or two. Whenever you or Tobias are going into the city."

"I will be glad to do that." With a curt nod, he hurried down the street toward his shop.

She shook her head as she watched him striding away. Would she ever understand Nathan? That man needed a wife. His wife had been gone several years, yet he had not remarried. He had many good qualities—a gentle nature, hard-working, and as she considered it, not an unattractive man. Yet he continued to live alone. Perhaps an unhappy marriage had soured him on taking another wife. She knew of one or two women who had looked his way with interest, but he resisted any overtures. Even the village matchmaker had thrown up her hands in frustration.

"How can one deal with such a man!" the woman had lamented.

How indeed, Martha mused.

As the day progressed, Martha began to consider how she would manage. Neighbors would help with the flax harvest, but who would sow the crops? Lazarus had done that. She and Mary had made goat cheese and the date cakes together. In time there would be the grape harvest and the figs to pick. Then there was the wine. She could not make it all by herself.

All her life she had been the capable one, planning, organizing, taking charge after their father died. Then she had Lazarus, young and strong, to handle the hard tasks. She eased herself down on the bench in the shade and felt herself torn between anger that her family would leave her like this and feeling more vulnerable than she had ever been in her life.

29

The second day after the Lord's appearing, she hoped for word from Thomas and Mary, but there was none. Martha began her daily task of sweeping the courtyard, still musing over Nathan's strange behavior. She realized he could not come and join the family for dinner anymore. There was no family, just herself. It wouldn't be proper.

Nathan had been such a loyal friend to the family through the years. Somehow appearing when they seemed to need him the most. She thought back to the incident with Thaddeus.

Lazarus told her Nathan thought she was in trouble when she ran into the olive grove, and then he'd seen her with Thaddeus. He'd been curt with her after that and left for Capernaum for several months. If she didn't know better, she'd think he was jealous . . .

She paused in her sweeping as a curious thought edged its way into her mind. He'd been a friend of her father's, though half his age; a friend to Lazarus, like an older brother, and while he was careful to follow decorum, always there. She remembered that once when Jesus was teaching and Nathan had come to listen, she caught him looking at her. An innocent look to be sure, but something else. He'd looked away quickly but not before she'd seen the wistful look on his face. She was busy serving as usual and didn't think any more about it, but now other scenes began to take their places in her mind.

She sat down suddenly on the bench as realization dawned. Was she the reason for Nathan's reluctance to choose another wife? Had she been so busy running her household she hadn't considered that he might have feelings for her? That he was too shy to present himself, or felt she wouldn't be interested?

Turning the thoughts over and over in her mind as one examines a coin, she contemplated her feelings for Nathan. Just a friend of the family? A big brother? She was always glad of his comforting presence. She felt safe when Nathan was around.

She liked him. Waving a hand in the air, she got up. This was foolishness. There was work to be done. She'd let her mind rattle on long enough.

She went to the storeroom and brought out a basket of wheat kernels, then sat down on a mat on the ground and poured the kernels into the small rotary mill she used for grinding. It felt good to move the wheel, giving her a sense of accomplishment as the flour began to appear. When she had enough flour for the bread, she added water and yeast and began to knead the dough.

She built up the fire in the mud brick oven and set the loaves to rise. She'd made the usual two loaves, and now as she looked at her work, she realized she only needed daily bread for one person, herself.

Her thoughts strayed to Nathan again. He would be restricted in coming to the house with no one else there. She had counted on his help with Lazarus gone. Even though he was a longtime friend of the family, the situation had changed.

She slid the loaves into the oven. If Nathan was interested, he'd had plenty of time to speak up. She shook her head. This was nonsense. She was imagining things just because she was lonely. The matchmaker was persistent, and in time she'd wear Nathan down and find a wife for him. Then he would certainly not be able to be of any help to her.

She chided herself for letting her fears run rampant. Only the God Who Sees knew what he had in store for her. Did he not know her coming and going? Having settled the matter in her mind, she went to water the garden and take an inventory of the storeroom.

That afternoon there was a knock on the gate and Nathan once again stood in front of her. "Peace be unto this house."

He shifted from one foot to the other but was obviously uncomfortable. Martha understood his dilemma and smiled up at him encouragingly.

"Will you come in and sit down? Can I bring you some refreshment?"

"Uh, no, I came to . . ."

"Yes?"

"I, uh, came to see if you had any weavings to go into the city."

"I don't have anything completed as yet, Nathan."

He rocked back on his heels. "Uh, yes, I forgot."

"Was there something else?"

He scratched his head. "Uh, do you have news of Mary and Thomas?"

What was the matter with Nathan today? It was not like him to come to their home without a purpose. "No, I've not had any word."

He pondered that thought. "I was wondering, what will you do now? Will Lazarus return?"

"I don't know. Lazarus might be able to return

when things quiet down, but not until the danger to him has passed. I don't know how long that will be. I am hoping that when whatever the Lord asked the believers to wait for has come, Mary and Thomas will come back here. The Lord's admonishment was to go into all the world. I don't know what they will do from there."

"You will be alone. That is not good."

"I can do little about it, Nathan. I must trust God to show me what to do. There are many in our village who have become believers." Since she had not given this any thought, she was surprised at the next words that tumbled from her mouth. "I was thinking that we could meet together, to pray and strengthen one another."

The idea seemed to appeal to him. He nodded his head. "Yes, that is a good idea." He looked down at her and there was something in his eyes. "You are a good woman, Martha, given to hospitality. I think the Lord would be pleased."

"Would you come, Nathan?"

"Yes, and others in the village would come."

He shifted from one foot to another. What was bothering him?

"I must get back to my shop. Goodbye." He backed away a few steps.

"Wait, Nathan," she said suddenly and went to get one of the loaves she'd baked. She handed it to him.

"Thank you." He looked at the bread as if it

were a wondrous gift, then turned abruptly and hurried down the street.

She stood at the gate, puzzled. Then, tired of doing household tasks, she picked up the basket and went out to the garden plot. It was a beautiful spring day. The morning glories grew in profusion around the fields and mixed in with them the deep blue of the pentagonias, imparting a blue tint to the ground around them. Early tulips had pushed their magnificent red flowers up from ancient bulbs. She picked some and added them to her basket. A little color around the house would be cheerful.

As she took in the beauty all around her, a sense of longing welled up in her again. She wanted . . . what was it? She wanted family around her again, someone to cook for, to hear laughter and voices in the courtyard again.

In the garden she picked some leeks and garlic, and a cucumber. The pomegranates beckoned to her from the tree, and she put two in her basket.

The day passed with still no word from Jerusalem, and she ate a quick supper, cleaned up the platter, and banked the fire in the small clay stove. There was nothing else she wanted to do, so she sat in the courtyard, saying her final prayers of the day, remembering Lazarus, the disciples, and Thomas and Mary.

Tomorrow she had decided to go and visit the home of Simon. Judith was a good friend, and

Tobias's wife, Chloe, was expecting another child. They would welcome her.

As she walked toward the gate to secure it, there was a firm knock and a voice called out, "Peace be upon this house." It was Zilpah, the village matchmaker.

30

Martha opened the gate and stared at Zilpah, then remembered her manners. "Come in. May I fix you some refreshment?"

"Perhaps a cup of . . . ?" Zilpah looked at her hopefully.

Martha for once was flustered. What could Zilpah possibly want here, now? Did she know about the wedding or had she come to speak to her about Mary?

She went to the storeroom and got a small wineskin, pouring the wine carefully into a wooden cup. She took some cheese from the stone crock. Placing the cheese on a small platter, she set the cup of wine in front of Zilpah and waited. Knowing the woman, she would get around to the purpose of her visit in her own time.

Perhaps if I help her along, Martha thought. "Mary is not here at present, Zilpah."

"I didn't come to present a proposal to Mary."

Zilpah gave her a sly look and almost purred. "I came to present a proposal of marriage . . . to you."

Martha sat down suddenly on the bench. "To me? But I am . . ."

"Yes, yes, past the most marriageable age. But I have been approached by a worthy man of the village. Naturally, under your circumstances— your brother gone and your sister off with . . ."

"She is with friends in Jerusalem, Zilpah. She has not run off. She is wed to Thomas."

Zilpah's eyes widened. "I did not know this." Zilpah prided herself on knowing everything that went on in Bethany. She recovered her composure. "Well, that is another matter." She waved a hand dismissing Mary for the moment. "As I said, it is you I have come to see. Now you realize you cannot be choosy at this time of your life."

Martha resisted a comment and kept her lips tightly closed.

Zilpah went on. "This man is a widower, no children, and has a good business so he is able to provide for your household. He would be a fine husband." She paused for effect.

"Who is this man who is asking for me, Zilpah?"

"None other than our blacksmith, Nathan."

Martha could not contain her astonishment. "Nathan? Why has he not said anything to me? He has been a friend of the family for a long time."

Zilpah reached over and patted her condescendingly on the knee. "My dear, you are a woman alone. Your father is dead, your brother has gone off to who knows where . . . to whom would he present himself?"

Nathan. Yes, he would want to do things in a proper way. Zilpah was right. He couldn't just walk into her courtyard and ask her to marry him. That was not the custom of her people. Thaddeus, a Gentile, might have felt free to say those things, but Nathan was a Jew and she could see that he felt Zilpah was the way he needed to go.

"I understand, Zilpah."

The woman gathered herself together and stood up. "Thank you for the refreshment. May I take an answer back to Nathan? As a family friend, of course, he felt sorry for you in your circumstances. It is a kind offer he makes, and a generous one."

Kind offer? In her circumstances? Martha kept her temper. The woman was insufferable. What did Zilpah know of Martha's needs? She didn't want someone who felt sorry for her. If that was his motive, he could keep his offer.

Out loud she said, "This is indeed kind of Nathan. I will consider his proposal and give him an answer tomorrow."

Zilpah huffed. "Seems to me there is little to think about. You need a man to help you. Nathan is willing."

Martha escorted the matchmaker to the gate and thanked her kindly for coming. When Zilpah had gone, she went back and sat on the bench, looking up at the sunset that painted the sky with glorious red, orange, and gold. Is this what she must settle for? Someone being kind to her? Torn between frustration and reality, she finally lay down on her pallet and cried out to the One who knew her heart.

A sense of peace filled her heart as she prayed, knowing that in Jesus she was fulfilled. He had shown her the love of God. It was his strength saw the kind face of her Lord in her mind and the gentle eyes of love that had changed her life. He was with her still.

The next morning she ate some bread and fruit and let her mind run with all the possibilities of Nathan's offer. She had always been a practical woman, and now she must think of more than herself. She had fields to tend, trees to reap from, and it was more than she could handle herself. There was no way of knowing how long Lazarus would be gone; indeed, he may not return at all.

There was a knock at the gate and she went to answer it, annoyed that Zilpah would return for her answer so soon. When she opened the gate, the words she intended to say died on her lips. It was Nathan.

"I thought it was Zilpah," Martha murmured

lamely. She wasn't sure what she wanted to say to Nathan right now.

He stepped into the courtyard, just inside the gate and searched her face. "I am aware that Zilpah presented my proposal, but when she returned and told me what she said to you, I realized she gave you the wrong reasons."

"Wrong reasons? Nathan, I appreciate that you felt the need out of kindness to provide for me, that you felt even a duty to—"

His voice was soft. "Woman, it was not for pity or duty. That's why I came. You could not know the feelings I have had for a long time. Your kind heart, your care of your father, all touched me more than I can tell you. I would have spoken sooner, but the Roman soldier convinced me that you could not care for me. When he was killed, I felt your grief. You have considered me only a friend of the family. I do not wish to just be a friend."

At her startled look, he shook his head quickly. "I mean, I wish to be more than a friend." He took a deep breath and sputtered. "It is not for pity that I wish you to be my wife."

He looked so relieved that the words were out and so like a lovesick schoolboy that suddenly joy bubbled up inside her, filling her up and spilling from her eyes. How had she been so blind?

She looked up into his face and there saw all the love and tenderness her heart had been longing for. He raised his bushy eyebrows in question as he waited for her to speak.

"I would be honored to be your wife, Nathan."

Suddenly he cried out, "I am the most fortunate of men!" In his exuberance, he picked her up and swung her around once before realizing what he'd done. He set her down quickly, embarrassed by his show of emotion.

She laughed then, and reaching up, put a hand on his cheek. He covered it with his own and they stood smiling at each other as a small breeze swirled the leaves around their feet.

Acknowledgments

Many thanks to Joyce Hart, my friend and agent, for your belief in me over the years and your persistence in finding a place for my work.

To my editor, Lonnie Hull DuPont, for her enthusiastic reception of *Journey to the Well* and now *Martha*. Thank you for all your encouraging words.

To the ladies of my Spiritual Life Book Club, thank you for all your prayers and support over the years and for your joyful thumbs-up on *Martha*.

Last but not least, thank you to my dear husband, Frank, who patiently puts up with my long hours on the computer and my one-track mind as I immerse myself in research.

Diana Wallis Taylor is an award-winning author, poet, and songwriter. *Journey to the Well* debuted in 2009, as did her Christian romance, *Smoke Before the Wind.* Her collection of poetry, *Wings of the Wind*, came out in 2007. A former teacher, she retired in 1990 as director of conference ser-vices for a private college. After their marriage in 1990, she and her husband moved to northern California where she fulfilled a dream of owning a bookshop/coffeehouse for writers' groups and poetry readings and was able to devote more time to her writing.

The Taylors have six grown children between them and ten grandchildren. They now live in the San Diego area, where between writing projects Diana is an inspirational speaker for Stonecroft Ministries, participates in Christian Women's Fellowship, serves on the board of the San Diego Christian Writer's Guild, and is active in the music ministry of her church. She enjoys teach-ing poetry and writing workshops, and sharing her heart with women of all ages.

Visit Diana's website at
www.dianawallistaylor.com.

Center Point Publishing
600 Brooks Road ● PO Box 1
Thorndike ME 04986-0001 USA

(207) 568-3717

US & Canada:
1 800 929-9108
www.centerpointlargeprint.com